COPY <|> PASTE and other stories

Derin Edala

Published by Derin Edala, 2024.

COPY <|> PASTE AND OTHER STORIES

First edition. September 7, 2024.

ISBN: 979-8227133618

Written by Derin Edala.

Table of Contents

COPY<|>PASTE 1: Copykate.. 1
COPY<|>PASTE 2: Post-Scarcity Society.......................31
COPY<|>PASTE 3: Intrapersonal Conflict 53
Wasting Time 75
Original Sin..81
Isolation Hysteria..87
Angel 91
World Builder..97
Unknown Complications 107
How To Escape The Well..111

COPY<|>PASTE 1: Copykate

KATE-1

Waking up inside a cramped, dark metal box is somehow even more disconcerting the second time.

There are extenuating circumstances, I suppose. The first time I'd done this, I was full of excitement and optimism about my new job as the head foldgate tech on an entirely new planet, and while I had been a bit apprehensive about climbing into an actual fold-shielded transport crate for the rickety journey through a foldgate built with tech a full century older than I was instead of the smooth, instant journeys I was used to, I was too eager to get going to be properly apprehensive, and my destination was too busy for me to sit in the box and stress out all that much. Whereas this second journey, taking place nearly two years after the ancient gate's foldfield had unexpectedly collapsed, stranding six of us over eighty light years from Earth with limited supplies and no hope of ever re-establishing contact, is in somewhat more harrowing circumstances. My five companions are long dead, meaning that there's no particular rush to get up before properly reflecting on my situation, and the fact that I made this journey through a collapsed foldgate isn't helping.

Also, there's a bunch of dirt in the box with me that wasn't here when I went in. I'm not sure what that means but it's probably really bad.

Fortunately, I'm a fucking genius. I mean, I'm *by definition* the best foldgate tech on the planet, so. That has to count for something. Right?

The absurdly outdated tech of our foldgate was mandated by simple physics. Sure, we had long ago mastered instant travel; I could step out of my dormitory on Earth and into a bar on the moon for no cost higher than a few hundred ditting and some motion sickness induced by the sudden gravity change (a fair price to pay considering that low gravity was the best for getting absolutely pissed in), but that's because foldgates already exist in those locations. Going to a planted ninety lightyears away means transporting the gate ninety lightyears through normal physical space, subject to the twin tyrants of fuel capacity and time. My great-grandparents hadn't been born when this gate was originally built.

Which is absolutely fantastic news for me, and the entire reason I've just travelled through a disconnected foldgate that can only take me to the location I started in; a poorly maintained giant dome on a faraway planet featuring one (1) living colonist.

See, here's the thing about old foldgates: they're absurdly inefficient. A modern gate, you step in, you step out, it's all smooth, no problem. You don't need to be crammed in a shielded box or lose any time; they transmit your data and matter perfectly through the fold with very few, and very rare, errors. Old gates? Nothing like that. They hadn't figured out informational efficiency in transmitting string field data when this thing was built. It does the job with about the same rate of accuracy, but it's messy. It's bulky. It holds too much data for too long, and now that the fold gate's collapsed, it has nothing to do with that data except feed it back to itself. What's the point of a fold gate that just pulls you apart, moves you really inefficiently in a tiny circle, and puts you back together again?

No point at all, if your goal is transport. But if you're a foldgate tech very highly trained on modern methods of packing data, given unrestricted access to an ancient beefy piece of shit that technology abandoned a century ago but was, at least, designed to deal with vast amounts of inefficiently packed data that required external shielding, in an environment completely free of most distractions and in a desperate race for your own survival, and, let's be honest, an absolute fucking genius, you start to think outside the foldfield.

Or more specifically, very much inside the foldfield. Specifically, the data inside the foldfield. 'Cause do you know what we call transport that doesn't go anywhere?

Storage.

The error-ridden mess of a machine currently towering over my little metal box (I assume, I can't see it right now) was a real deathbee to work with, but honestly, failure wasn't an option. The foldfield had collapsed before any living supplies were brought through; we hadn't had any seeds to grow, any algae to farm. We had stored, sterile food, and we had carbon and hydrogen and oxygen and the other trace elements necessary for life, and we had energy to store in it in our nuclear reactor, but no little living biomachines to turn it into life we could eat and gain that energy from. So I'd had to make my own machine, before time ran out. A foldgate picks up what goes into it, transmits the material and the data of the position of all its little bits relative to the rest to another foldgate via the field, and then it comes out the other end 'dentical, more or less, to how it went in. Then it's done. But what if you looped a foldfield from one gate to itself (the only option I'd had, way out here), and transmitted the data round and round indefinitely? That's stored data. A stored pattern.

And what if you broke a bunch of the safeties so that the data kept going round after you built it at the other end?

And what if you broke more safeties so that matter could be accepted into the field without storing the necessary data, and instead copying it from other data still in transit? Then you don't have a transport machine at all. You have a copy machine.

According to my calculations, there should be enough energy in the foldfield to store roughly nine thousand patterns. That's far, far more than I need. I had transported every kind of food I had, clean water, and oxygen, and lived alone for nearly a year letting the foldgate and the nuclear reactor take control of pretty much all of my life support before realising I could push things further.

This is a big dome, that I live in. It's a very lonely dome. And even with the foldgate taking care of so much, the dome requires far, far more maintenance than one person has the time to give it.

So that's why I'm in here. Transporting myself, to make copies later. Putting my data into the foldfield, to cycle around and around and let me make as many Kates as I need.

So you can see why I'm apprehensive. I had to break so many safeties on this thing, and its ability to deal with simple matter doesn't guarantee that it can handle me. I'm not stupid; I ran as many living tests as I could, but as I've said, life is pretty rare out here. It's me and the bacteria that came on our bodies. I cultured up some of those and ran them through and observed them for several days, but a human's a shipload more complicated than a microbe.

I... seem to be fine. Except the dirt. I'm not happy about the dirt. That wasn't in the box when I went in, meaning there's something wrong with the data, meaning there could be all kinds of shit inside me. I'm going to have to run as many medical tests as possible. As soon as possible.

I push the lid of the metal box up and go to climb out into the empty, desolate transport room.

It's not empty.

The young woman at the control terminal looks like she hasn't slept in days. She peers dimly at me with bloodshot brown eyes under limp, tangled chestnut hair plastered to her head in some places and sticking out in others. The usual bouncy curls hang in greasy helical strings. Her eyes are so heavily shadowed that the sockets look bruised against her pale skin, and she has the look of someone who's usually pretty well-filled-out but has missed multiple recent meals. Even her orange jumpsuit doesn't look clean. Her eyes widen as I emerge – not with shock or surprise, she was clearly expecting me – but widen, nonetheless.

"Holy fucking whalepiss," she breathes. "I can't believe that worked."

Also, she looks exactly like me. I mean. Obviously. Everyone else is dead, remember?

I'm still adjusting to the situation as I clamber out of the box. I can't believe I didn't consider this possibility; I mean, the dirt in the box is a dead giveaway. If I'd been the original, going through the foldgate to make the copy data, then the gate would be building me out of the material that entered it; nothing lost, nothing gained. But when building a copy out of random materials, it's better to oversupply than undersupply, lest your clone come out missing whatever there wasn't enough matter to build. So, obviously, there'd be a few extra scoops of raw matter left in the box. I used to get leftovers when I was first experimenting with copying food this way, too.

Original Kate rushes over to help me, supporting my arms as I step out. "Look at you!" she breathes. "You're beautiful!"

"I look like you, and you look like shit," I point out.

She laughs. "But my genius is beautiful, and you're a creation of my genius, ergo you must be, also. How are you feeling? We need to do, like, so many health tests."

"What about you?" I ask. "You clearly came out alright."

"Oh, that was days ago. I've run every medical test I can on myself, but it's more risky for you. Because of the – "

"Because the foldfield's been cycling the information around for awhile, yeah. Well, apparently it can handle it, even information this complicated. We are so fucking clever. Am I the first?"

"Yes. I'm thinking that once we've confirmed that you're successfully copied, we should fire it up again and make – "

"Nine more, yes, I remember running the efficiency calculations."

"So."

"So."

We look at each other.

I crack my knuckles. "A whole bunch of medical tests, and then..."

She cracks her knuckles. "And then, we get to work."

· · · ·

KATE-6

Waking up inside a cramped, dark metal box is somehow even more disconcerting the second time.

There are extenuating circumstances, I suppose. My five companions are long dead, meaning there's no particular rush to get up before properly reflecting on my situation, and the fact that I made this journey through a collapsed foldgate isn't helping.

Also, there's a bunch of dirt in the box with me that wasn't here when I went in. I'm not sure what that means but it's probably really bad.

Fortunately, I'm a fucking genius. I mean, I'm *by definition* the best foldgate tech on the planet, so. That has to count for something. Right?

I... seem to be fine. Except the dirt. I'm not happy about the dirt. That wasn't in the box when I went in, meaning there's something wrong with the data, meaning there could be all kinds of shit inside me. I'm going to have to run as many medical tests as possible. As soon as possible.

I push the lid of the metal box up and go to climb out into the empty, desolate transport room.

It's not empty.

There are six women in the room, and except for the one standing next to the box and offering me a hand out, they're all ignoring me. They seem pretty relaxed about the situation, most of them typing away at computers. One of them sweeps the floor. They've certainly all showered and slept a lot more recently than I have.

They all look exactly like me. Obviously.

"Welcome to Kateland, population: Kate," the Kate over my box says as she helps me out. "Let's get some food and water in you and then we can get you your tasks."

"We need to make a new copy," one of the other Kates says.

"We are," another Kate says. "In fact, we're going to make –"

"Four more, yeah, that's not what I meant. I mean, one of us should go through and copy ourselves." She flicks her fingers at me. "Everyone comes out hungry and tired and disoriented, and then we have to help them recover and get them up to speed, which is a completely unnecessary waste of time. Why not copy someone who's well-rested and knows what's going on?"

"Who should we copy?" another Kate asks. "You?"

The first Kate shrugs. "Or you. Whoever's in the best physical condition, I guess. It doesn't matter. We've only been different people for a few days, it should all work out the same."

"Let's get Kate-6 up to normal," says the Kate helping me out of the box, "and then we can spin a bottle for it."

• • • •

KATE-3-4

There's dirt in the box when I wake up.

We've figured out the correct materials needed by now, of course, but we decided to keep putting extra in anyway – both for safety, and as an orienting aid. There's dirt, so I know I'm not the Kate who walked into this machine to make a foldfield copy. I'm the copy.

That's good information to have. Knowing what's going on in advance is all good information to have. Kate-4 was right;

this is much less disorienting than last time. We'd decided to copy new Kates from a few different existing Kates, so if they kept the copy order the same, I should be the last of the initial ten off the line. The eleventh Kate to exist.

Maybe earlier, if they changed the copy order. It shouldn't matter, one way or the other. I push the box open.

There's a Kate there to help me out, of course. Orange jumpsuit, clean hair, alert expression. Everything I expect.

Well. Except for the fact that she looks *at least* a decade older than me. Little crow's feet in the eyes, grey streaks in the hair... yeah, this Kate is approaching forty.

Ah, there's the feeling of confusion and disorientation! I knew it had to be somewhere.

She offers me a hand. "Welcome to Kateopolis, population: Kate," she says, in the rote tone of someone who's said it many, many times before.

"We still haven't come up with a real name for this place?" I ask.

She leads me down the hall out of the transport room at a brisk pace. "We still haven't come up with a real name for this place. Now, to answer your next handful of questions: it's been fourteen years. Yes, I know I look good for my age, thank you. Yes, I'm also surprised we somehow managed to keep this total circus going for so long and aren't all dead yet. No, I'm not your Kate ancestor; I'm Kate-4. Yes, your Kate ancestor, Kate-3, is still alive. Yes, I know that from your perspective you and I were just having a conversation ten minutes ago, and yes this is weird. You're the fourth copy of Kate-3, and the third copy to be made recently. There are thirty nine Kates in Kateopolis. And the reason you exist is to be a doctor."

"A doctor? I don't know any more about medicine than I need to to alter the fold – "

"The foldgate, yes, I remember. We've got a couple of Kates who have dealt with medical issues who will teach you what they know, and we still have all the medical books and papers and stuff that Reginald brought with him."

I nod. Reginald was one of the colony doctors, the only doctor among the six of us who'd gotten through the foldgate before the foldfield had collapsed. He'd brought a huge amount of Earth's medical knowledge with him in digital form, because why not? Having local access to as much information as possible just made sense.

"If you have a medical problem, why not have a Kate who's picked up some medical knowledge already deal with it? Why get an entirely new one who doesn't know anything?"

"We don't have a medical problem. We're building doctors for when we do."

"... What?"

Kate-4 sighs impatiently. "Okay, so we can make as much of anything as we want so long as we have the power, the base material, and a base to copy it from, right? That includes experts. It makes no sense to just ad-hoc learn whatever we need on the spot when we have an expert-copying machine right there. So that's what we're making. We've decided to develop specialists in medicine, engineering, chemistry, and computer tech; then, if we need to, we can have as many experts as we need later on without having to train any new people. Now, one of us could do it, but the enemy here is time. All the foldgate tech in the world won't stop us from ageing, and it takes time to develop expertise. If one of us did it, we'd be on a totally unnecessary ten-year disadvantage; ten years older for the same level of experience and knowledge. It's best to start with a Kate as young as possible, and the Kate-3 copy data was determined to be the best candidate. So, you exist."

"And I don't get to pick my own speciality?"

"No point. All four of you are the same person right now, you'll all have the same speciality preferences. You drew medicine. So we want you to spend a year studying up on basic biology and medicine, as much as you can, and then we'll send you through the foldgate to store your data. Then you can branch out into whatever medical field you like the most, I guess, and we can send you through the foldgate again when you're good at it. As we need more specialists in different areas of medicine, we can make copies of our 'basic biology' Kate and get them to specialise differently. We're limited by how many resources this place can support at once, due to the power limitations of the reactor determining how much food we can print, but we should have a pretty solid repertoire of experts within a couple of generations."

"Oh, you're planning long term. You really think we'll survive that long?"

"Why not? We survived this long, the domes and machines were designed to support a full colony indefinitely, and don't forget, we're a fucking genius."

"Well. That is true."

As we walk out of the transport centre into the main dome, I can't help but gasp. The colony had been built (by labourers and their machines who'd come through, worked, and left before we colonists had started to arrive) with a lot of "open air" areas, big spaces between buildings all capped by giant domes to hold the breathable atmosphere in. Much more resource-intensive and difficult than simply connecting all the buildings together and making them into pressure vessels, but it had been deemed psychologically important for a large colony of people, most of them unlikely to return to Earth for years or even decades at a time, to be able to go "outside" and see the "sky". Admittedly the "sky" is a pure white with neither stars nor sun in sight, but you can look up and *almost* convince yourself it's just a really cloudy day.

Anyway, the last time I'd been out here, things hadn't been in the best shape. Nothing important had been broken, but years of a location designed for thousands of people being inhabited by six people that slowly dwindled to one hadn't made things like "keeping stuff pretty" a high priority. Dirt and damage don't accumulate very quickly in a tightly controlled atmosphere with almost no life in it, but what little dust had gathered had remained untouched, and there's been boxes of random supplies opened and scattered among the "streets" – with no weather to damage them, there was no need to store them carefully. The whole place had felt abandoned, because it mostly was.

That's no longer the case. The buildings immediately surrounding the transport centre have apparently been converted into living spaces, and the mess that surrounds them is the mess of life – overalls hanging on a clothesline to dry (even though there's no reason for them to dry faster outside the house than inside), any boxes are on the doorsteps, the streets are kept clear for foot traffic. Most of the dome is probably still abandoned except for necessary system maintenance, but here around the transport centre, it's alive.

"All the buildings close by should be furnished," Kate-4 says. "Pick one without a Kate in it and set up shop. I've gotta go and make us an engineer."

I nod. Time to get to work, I guess.

. . . .

KATE-3-5

"Hey." I hand a bag of chocolate-coated peanuts to the Kate tapping away at the computer next to me. "Eat something."

"You're not my mum," Kate-3-2 ("computer Kate") says, but she takes the proffered bag. Us four 'new Kates', the four printed to become specialists, tend to stick together – after only a month since printing, Kateopolis is still pretty disorienting, and I don't think the older Kates realise that. They've been building this place for a decade and a half; they're used to things, know how they work. They don't understand what it's like to go into a foldgate and wake up fourteen years in the future, surrounded by reflections of yourself who are all more competent and settled-in than you are.

"We need names," I say. "In eleven months, we're gonna copy our data to fork off prints into different specialisations, and we can't call each other 'computer Kate' and 'engineer Kate' when there's other IT specialists and engineers running around."

"Use the numbers then."

"I'm not calling anyone by a fucking serial number."

Computer Kate rolls her eyes, but I know she agrees with me. Of course she does; we're only separated by one month of time, we can't be that different. The numbers make sense for tracking copy threads, but not everyday use.

Sometimes it astounds me how different we are, or at least seem to be, after only one month of separation. Computer Kate is my favourite Kate, even though she should be nearly identical to me, Doctor Kate, and Chemist Kate. But she is different. I like the person I can be when I'm around her. There's something about her unwavering seriousness that makes me feel okay being lighthearted and silly, so long as she's there to pick up the slack on the serious side. And I haven't asked, but I think the feeling's mutual; she can focus on her serious, analytical side without feeling any pressure to be personable and try to lift the mood, when I'm around to do that.

"I think the older Kates have names," I say. "I mean, they'd have to by now, wouldn't they. I'm sure I heard one of them call another one Sunny yesterday."

A rare laugh from Computer Kate. "One of them named herself after our *childhood dog*?"

I shrug. "Who understands the deep mysteries of our mind once it's been matured for fourteen years in this fucking place? It's good to know that we can apparently last that long here and not want to kill each other. Gives me hope for the future."

"Mmm," Computer Kate says neutrally. I peek at her screen; she's apparently learning something about some new programming language. Well, presumably an old programming language that I don't know. The only programming I know how to do is directly related to foldgate operation, but Computer Kate needs to learn all the computer systems used throughout the dome, even though we're using very few of them (we can't farm, don't need to light or clean most of the space, and can replenish oxygen and clean water with the foldgate).

"So, if you don't want to be named after a dog, what should I call you?" I ask. "It is going to get confusing, when we have a whole bunch of Computer Kates running around."

"How many computer specialists do you think we'll need?"

"You never know."

"Counterpoint: it'll be even more confusing if we get names. Because then we'll end up with a bunch of Kates running around who all remember being named the same thing and aren't any more. Do you think it'd be any less confusing to have ten Kates running around all thinking their name is Dolly?"

"So you want to be called Dolly, then?"

"You want to be called Dolly."

"You can't prove that."

"Of course I can, Dolly. We're almost exactly the same person."

"You can be Dolly if you want," I allow.

"Nope. You're Dolly now."

I roll my eyes. "I bet one of the older Kates is Dolly. I bet they snapped up the name first thing."

"Fuck 'em."

• • • •

<u>KATE-3-2</u>

I've been alive for thirty years, but I've also been alive for eleven months. And in that eleven months, I've acquired the most important skill an IT specialist can have – I have mostly learned not to completely hate the computers. I'm going through the foldgate in one more month to make a copy of me to act as a template for future IT specialists, so if I can learn to like the computers by then, that'll certainly be advantageous.

Of us four "new Kates", I've often wondered how much of our differing personalities are just down to a general mood difference in having better or worse jobs. Dolly's our engineer, the closest field to our initial foldfield expertise, and is easily the most upbeat among us. Whereas our chemist is a total bitch.

"Hi, Sandy," Dolly calls, walking into my home without so much as a knock (as is her wont). I give her a wave without looking away from the computer. "You work too hard."

"You should be working hard. You're aware that we're in our last month before making the templates, right? Don't you want future engineers to have the best basis possible?"

She rolls her eyes. "They will, because I'm awesome at engineering. It's not my fault that you find computers so hard."

I get up and gesture to my seat. "You're welcome to do it."

"Ha, no. Anyway, if you take longer than the next month to be basically competent, you can always just make a new template later on. They only gave us a year so there'd be a deadline."

I slump back down into my seat. She sits on my lap, eyes trained on my screen.

"You're making it hard to get any work done," I point out.

"Ooooh nooo. You might have to take a break." She pushes her head forward to block my view of the screen. Her eyes rest on my lips for a second. She looks away, blushing.

She's been doing this for over six months now. She won't get over it and she won't make a move, and I'm just not that patient. So I kiss her.

The reaction is immediate. She pushes herself off my lap and scrambles away, cheeks aflame. "We can't!"

We can. But pushing won't help, so I just shrug. "Okay."

"I mean. Do you want to?"

"Have we ever kissed anyone we didn't want to kiss, Dolly?"

"The others won't stand for it."

"Fuck 'em."

"We can't just..."

"Dolly. There is no one else here. Only Kates. Do you intend to be alone for the rest of your life?"

"The... all the other Kates don't..."

"Some of them have been here for fifteen years. Do you really believe that?"

"They wouldn't..."

"What you and I want is proof that they would."

"I have to... go."

"Alright." I turn back to my work. I let her leave.

I can't concentrate on getting any work done.

• • • •

<u>KATE-3-3</u>

I look away from Dolly and Sandy in the corner giving each other lovey eyes, not bothering to hide my scowl. "It's disgusting," I tell the doctor. "They're so fucking shameless."

"Mm-hmm." She pours boiling water into her dehydrated meal pack and seals it up.

"Doesn't it piss you off? Doesn't it gross you out? Aren't you as disgusted as I am?"

"Yeah, obviously. But what do you want me to do about it?"

"Do about it? We've got this incest going on and we're just supposed to ignore it?"

"I don't think it's incest if it's yourself. I think that's just narcissism."

"Whatever! We can't just – "

"What do you want me to do about it? What can anybody do about it? Put them on opposite sides of the colony and not let them see each other? Or do you just want to follow them around with a spray bottle and squirt them any time they touch each other, like a cat? If they want to be weird and gross, that's their problem."

"I don't understand how you can be calm about this. I can't believe they would – "

"Or you can't believe *you* would?"

"I'd never!"

Doctor Kate gestures across the room at the pair with her fork. "Apparently, you would."

• • • •

<u>KATE-3-2</u>

"Does it work?" the chemist asks me, not bothering to disguise the sneer in her voice.

"What?"

"Your stupid little incest thing. Does it actually make you feel less lonely? Like you're not on a planet all by yourself with all of humanity an unreachable number of light years away?"

"A bit. Well. Not really. Does being a total bitch and picking constant fights with everyone make you feel less lonely?"

"Yes, actually."

I can't help but laugh disbelievingly. "Seriously?"

"Of course. It reminds me how different we are, if we disagree so much."

"And you need to feel different to me, don't you? You need to feel better than me."

"Oh, don't you fucking act like – "

"Excuse me. I have work to do."

• • • •

<u>KATE-3-5-1</u>

There's dirt in the box.

That means I'm not Dolly, then. Or, I'm not the Dolly who went through the foldgate to copy her data and was immediately reformed at the other end. I'm a copy, so I can expect some time to have passed. The last thing I remember doing was going in to make the basic template for new engineers, so that means I exist because the colony wants to train a new specialist engineer.

Okay.

I push up the lid of the box and am helped out by Kate-4, the foldgate manager, just like last time. I know it's her because she has a big patch on her jumpsuit that reads KATE-4, FOLDGATE MANAGER. Presumably to head off some of the repetitive new Kate questions. She looks essentially the same as last time I saw her, which is a little worrying. Why do they need a new engineer so soon? Maybe they're just being proactive, getting as many different kinds of specialists trained up and templated as possible. Just in case.

"Welcome to Kateopilis, popu – "

"Population: Kate, yeah, I know," I grumble as I let her help me up. I glance at the calendar on the wall. I only made – *Dolly* only made my template about two months ago. "Why do you need a new engineer so fast? Is there some kind of emergency?"

"Hard to say. There's been some... inconsistencies with the sensory hardware outside the dome. Dolly's been looking into it, but we need someone to take over more general engineering duties, so."

So that's me, then. That's... less jarring than any other option, actually. I'd been expecting to keep doing general engineering when I'd gone into the foldgate last, so picking up the same line of work coming out of it is good. It'll be difficult to adapt to a new name, difficult to adapt to being the fifth, youngest Young Kate, but I'll manage.

As we walk out of the transport room and out into the open dome, I see two Kates hanging out outside a house, and my heart freezes, because I know exactly who they are. One has her arms around the other's shoulders, and they're looking into each other's eyes, smiling. Then Dolly glances up and spots me.

"Oh, hey! Sandy, it's the new engineer!" She gives me a wave. "Welcome to Kateopolis!"

I wave back, a little uncertainly. She's looking at me like a friendly stranger, like I'm not her from just a couple of months ago. And then Sandy looks up, and looks at me with those calm yet piercing eyes that look like every other Kate's eyes but somehow oh so different, those eyes that she'd settled on me just five minutes ago when giving me a final kiss right before

I got into the transport crate, and looks at me happily, but politely. With a little nod.

And then she turns back to Dolly, and looks at her like she's the whole world.

I'm her! I want to scream. *I'm her from just two fucking months ago, and I'm nothing to you? What great intimate strides could you two have possibly made over just two months that makes me nothing to you by comparison?!*

"There's a free house over this way," Kate-4 says, leading me away from the couple, in the opposite direction to the house I remember living in for the past fucking year. I follow her as quickly as I can.

I have some feelings to feel, and I don't want to be feeling them in public.

• • • •

KATE-5

I'm crying in my space suit as I drag Kate-0 in through the airlock. We don't even cycle it properly, just let it pump air in until it makes up the difference between the thin outside atmosphere and the 1atm inside the dome. Any toxic outside atmosphere it lets in doesn't fucking matter, we can deal with that later. It doesn't fucking matter.

Not next to this.

Kate-0, the original Kate, the one who successfully stabilised the looped foldfield and lived a year getting it ready to make living copies and went through to copy her own data to create all of us and all of our copies, isn't breathing. She's not responding to anything I say, not moving in my grip, and her pulse is flat. It didn't seem to matter which Kates went out to check the external dome equipment, so we just sent the two of us with the most out-of-dome experience. It didn't seem to matter, until the seals on her suit failed, and we were way too far away from the airlock.

I drag her into the dome proper and we're immediately surrounded by other Kates, ripping her helmet off, dragging her out of her suit, starting CPR. We have three doctors now and all of them are present, and the fact that all of them have had time to beat us here tells me that getting back inside took way too long. There's no chance.

Kates take turns doing CPR anyway. Some Kates exchange glances with me, ask if I'm okay. But I can't help but wonder if they wish I'd died instead.

It's what I would wish, in their situation. A Kate is a Kate is a Kate, and it's frankly amazing that we've gone so long without a death; we'd expected to lose some eventually. I hadn't realised that it would hurt so much to specifically lose her.

We weren't even that close, is the thing. I didn't know her that well, beyond the twenty nine years of life memories I shared with all Kates. But she was, in ways I'd never really considered, kind of our link to Earth. Our original. The Kate who'd stood on Earth soil, once, and come here, and made us.

Which is a stupid nonsense perspective. When you step through a foldgate, your matter is all squished up, and reassembled at the other end. You could argue that we 'die' and are revived every time we use a foldgate, so what makes her more of the person that stepped in than me? Because she was printed first, out of the same physical matter that went in? That's a stupid distinction. Carbon is carbon and hydrogen is hydrogen; why does it matter if it comes from deconstructed cells or deconstructed soil? Besides, cells change, die, get replaced over time, and it's been twenty years – her bones are probably still made of the same calcium as the bones that stepped in the foldgate on Earth, but most of her, like the rest of us, is made of food replicated here, from matter that was brought from Earth in a decidedly not human form. There's no distinction, no *real* distinction, that makes Kate-0 more of an 'original' than me or any other Kate around me.

But it feels like there is.

An unbroken line of continuity, a woman who stepped into a gate on Earth and walked out here, of the same flesh. Who built the rest of us out of soil and lived among us as one of us; we'd certainly never bothered to make any distinction when she was alive. A Kate was a Kate was a Kate. But looking at her lifeless on the ground, I can only feel that she was THE Kate. Something precious, lost forever.

An unbroken line of continuity... broken. From the grief and worry and desperation in the eyes around me, I know that the other Kates are experiencing something similar.

And then someone's eyes widen in realisation. She looks up, catches the eyes of another Kate, who just looks confused... but another Kate's eyes widen, too. A third Kate, a fourth.

And then I realise. Everything clicks together, and I know what we're about to do.

We're about to do something irrational and stupid.

. . . .

<u>KATE-7</u>
Waking up inside a cramped, dark metal box is somehow even more disconcerting the second time.

There are extenuating circumstances, I suppose. My five companions are long dead, meaning there's no particular rush to get up before properly reflecting on my situation, and the fact that I made this journey through a collapsed foldgate isn't helping.

Also, there's a bunch of dirt in the box with me that wasn't here when I went in. I'm not sure what that means but it's probably really bad.

Fortunately, I'm a fucking genius. I mean, I'm *by definition* the best foldgate tech on the planet, so. That has to count for something. Right?

I... seem to be fine. Except the dirt. I'm not happy about the dirt. That wasn't in the box when I went in, meaning there's something wrong with the data, meaning there could be all kinds of shit inside me. I'm going to have to run as many medical tests as possible. As soon as possible.

I push the lid of the metal box up and go to climb out into the empty, desolate transport room.

It's not empty.

"Welcome to Kateopolis," the older woman standing over me says, giving me a gentle smile. "Population: Kate."

She looks like me (obviously, there's no one else here), except about fifty years old. My first thought is a somewhat delirious, 'oh, I guess it took a really long time to perfect this tech, then'. But the badge sewn into her uniform reads KATE-4, FOLDGATE MANAGER, suggesting some level of organisation. And at least four other Kates.

She gives me a brief rundown of Kateopolis, how things work and what to expect, as she helps me out of the box and we head outside. There are a lot of Kates, some general labourers, some specialists. A doctor, if I need medical attention. There's a house all ready for me to move in, and she gives me the address of a Kate to go to who can arrange anything else I might need.

"So what's my job, then?" I ask.

"Oh, whatever comes up. We can fit you into the general labour roster easily enough; patrolling for problems, that sort of thing."

They made me for no reason? "You just... felt like making a new Kate?"

Kate-4 shrugs. "We recently lost a Kate. It's good to keep the numbers stable. For inventorying purposes.

That... kind of makes sense... I guess. I follow Kate-4, let her show me the bar and the common eating area and the supply depot, then escort me to my new house. The last time I saw this place, yesterday (twenty years ago yesterday), it had been a reception building, but everywhere around the foldgate has been turned into a living space now. It's well-furnished and tidy, and very close to the foldgate (amazing it wasn't already taken.) It's a good place.

It takes me about a day to realise that something is really, really wrong with this place.

Most notably, everyone is so *nice* to me. That's fucking weird. These people are me and I'm not nice. I'll walk into a room containing two Kates having a good long bitch about a third Kate and suddenly they're all smiles and hellos and answering any questions I have as nicely and gently as possible. Nobody seems overly keen about making sure I'm actually on any work roster, which is fine, I guess everything's already handled, but why make another Kate if you don't have work that needs doing? More Kates means more food and water production via the foldgate, more power being used by the reactor, more work for the oxygenation system, just generally more labour and fuss. Not a huge amount, but why make extra work for no reason?

Also, there are no Kates my age. Both in terms of, no one is twenty nine, and no one has been printed recently. The most recently printed Kate I can find was printed two years before me. A lot of the older Kates are talking about how over the next few years they're going to get too old to do quite so much physical work, and they'll need new, younger Kates, but they haven't started making those, yet. Maybe I'm a sort of test run, a preliminary younger Kate? No; that doesn't make sense. There's no reason to do that.

What am I *for*?

Foldgate tech is what I know, what I'm good at, so I start helping out Kate-4 with the foldgate in my spare time, and no one stops me. After a little while, while we load canisters of carbon dioxide into the foldgate to turn them into oxygen canisters and graphite, I'm able to needle an explanation out of her.

"I told you how we lost a Kate recently, right?" she says. "Well, she was Kate-0. The original. It's hitting everyone pretty hard."

"Okay, but you know that doesn't actually mean anything, right? I mean, death sucks, but the 'original' part. She wasn't any diff – "

"Yes, we know that, but it still feels... well. I don't want to depress you, but after awhile, living here on a dead end world surrounded only by echoes of yourself and with the persistent knowledge that you're too far from anywhere and too dependent on a single life support dome to actually built any civilisation that can actually go anywhere, knowing you're just running down an invisible clock alone until something breaks, can get a little... wearing."

I nod. I've only been here a week and I'm already getting that impression. I remember the years before being printed all too well; the desperate race for survival, for a food source in altering the foldgate, and, during the monotony of food security and routine maintenance tasks with a terrifyingly long, lone future stretching out ahead of me, for company.

"What's that got to do with me, though?" I ask. "I'm not her."

"Well... yes," Kate-4 admits. "You are."

I almost drop the canister I'm holding. I stare down at the box we're loading, then back up at her. She nods.

"We had her body," she explains. "We just needed to put life back into it. So we put it in the foldgate and printed from the only template we had of her. Which is the first one."

"There was... there was dirt in the box when I woke up," I point out.

"Well, yes. She'd lost a fair bit of weight towards the end of her life; we needed to be sure that there was enough matter to make you. Honestly, I was a little worried; if the foldfield had used all the dirt first and left bits of the body in there, your awakening could've been... unpleasant."

I shudder at the thought. "You never made another template of the original Kate?"

She shrugs. "It never seemed necessary? We make templates of people when we have a reason to replicate them. Most of them are from second generation copies, our specialists. She – you – mostly did general labour, like most of us older Kates. There was no reason to replicate; we didn't... we didn't really think it was important, until you were gone."

"I'm not her," I say firmly, even though I am. But what I mean is, I'm not any more her than the other Kates.

"No? Do you remember doing it? Altering the gate, running the microbe experiments, climbing into the box and just hoping you'll make it out of the other end alive, willing to take the risk because the alternative is a life alone all the way out – "

"You remember that, too! We all did that!"

"I'm sure you remember it more clearly than me."

"Yes, because I'm a lot younger! It was just last week for me! That's going to be true of any Kate you print from an early template, not just me. I'm not going to be anyone's mascot!"

Kate-4 looks at me sadly. "I don't think either you or I really have much of a say in that."

Life in the colony continues. People keep treating me extra gently, and knowing why just makes it more frustrating. It's little things; more patience, more consideration. An absolute refusal to let me do anything dangerous, which is just fucking patronising. I learn pretty quickly that most of the other Kates have new names, probably to avoid confusion. Some don't; some just go by 'the doctor' or 'green-door Kate' or whatever, but most of them call themselves something new. Kate-4 explains that she still goes by Kate-4 mostly to avoid confusion with new prints. "It's a lot less confusing if new Kates can see who I am in relation to them immediately," she explains, tapping the name sewn into her jumpsuit. "And I'd rather just keep the same name everywhere."

Nobody, ever, even suggests calling me anything other than 'Kate'. Even when I start introducing myself as Kate-7, they won't say it.

Kateopolis is... well. To be honest, I don't know how so many Kates have survived for two decades in this place. They have their hobbies and their distractions, making art or whatever, but it's all just me talking to myself, isn't it? There's no point to any of it, it's so unbearably lonely. It takes me a while to realise why I'm handling it worse than they are; none of them will talk to me, not properly. Oh, we'll have conversations. But they don't disagree, don't argue, don't snap at me even when 'm being a total bitch on purpose. They're just smiling reflections of me, of various ages. I've often wondered if the kind of absurdly powerful people with no real friends are ever lonely, surrounded by yes-men; it sounds like the loneliest fate one could have. Well, I've found one that's even lonelier. Being surrounded by yes-reflections.

I look at them, and I can't see them, because they won't let me. They look at me, and I know they don't see me, either. But they don't see me as a reflection of them; they see me as her. Their talisman, their pretend unbroken chain connecting them to an Earth that none of us will ever see again. I exist to be a coping mechanism, and I don't think it's even worth telling them that I'm not coping.

One morning, I glare at my own reflection in the mirror for ten minutes. This is, somehow, less lonely than going outside; at least my reflection will glare back. I can have an argument with my reflection; I can pretend there's someone on the other side more than I can if I go outside and talk to real people.

I glare at my reflection for a bit longer, and then I go and get a knife. I make sure it's sharp and clean, and I bring a first aid kit with me to clean up after. The last thing I want is an infection.

I think it might help, see, if I make it so the other Kates look less like reflections of me.

And I think it might help, see, if they can look at me and see someone who looks irreconcilably different from the Kate they want to pretend I am.

I set the knife blade to my cheek and, very carefully, I get to work.

COPY<|>PASTE 2: Post-Scarcity Society

KATE-3-5-2-1

"So, how are you liking life in a post-scarcity society?" Ruby asks, slumping down in a seat across from me in the mess hall. She's an older Kate than me by about two years, and a doctor, an oncologist in training preparing for a foreseen need of the older Kates needing one soon, but she finds excuses to get involved in my engineering work. I don't mind; engineering is way more interesting than biology, and I was only printed a couple of months ago and am still adjusting to the time skip, so it's nice to have someone to help.

"This is hardly a post-scarcity society," I remark, poking at my freeze dried dinner while I wait for it to rehydrate properly.

"We have a magic printer! Whatever we want, we can – "

"Whatever we already have to scan in," I point out. "We can make a lot of a very limited range of things." I scowl at my food. Although, to be fair, the past couple of decades' worth of Kates have made wondrous strides in the food variety department. With nothing to grow, there's little to be done to expand the repertoire, but one thing we Kates are great at doing is pushing boundaries. Mostly through food separation – chocolate peeled carefully off chocolate-coated nuts and put through the foldgate separately gives us chocolate and nuts. The little spice packs in instant noodles had their ingredients separated grain by grain into individual spices, to be replicated up and remixed in different ways for variety. Chemists devoted their free time to synthesising simple artificial flavourings and food scents; most of them are a little too complex to make in the facilities we have, but you can do a lot with a few synthesised salts and esters. One of the doctors drew some of her blood to make blood pudding, which is so much more soft and succulent than the dehydrated foods we have available and feels almost like eating real fresh meat.

Whenever a Kate dies, there's some talk of putting *real* fresh meat on the menu, but nobody's made that copy, at least to my knowledge. It feels like going a bit too far.

"You," Ruby tells me, "are a killjoy. I was so much more optimistic at your age."

"To think, you had the full potential within you to be like me, and you chose to be like you instead. How embarrassing for you."

"Can you imagine what Earth would do with this tech? Maybe they have it by now. I mean, we're not the *only* genius foldgate technician in existence, surely. And there's got to be an old foldgate with all the space and the shielding for old clunky foldfield tech in a museum somewhere, so maybe someone..."

"Earth would have no use for this," I point out. "It's a matter of energy efficiency. Using a foldgate normally doesn't take much energy, but what we're doing sure as fuck does. We're sitting on top of a giant nuclear power generator designed to support a colony of, eventually, ten or twenty thousand people, and we're already hitting limits at less than two hundred of us. Part of that is that it takes time to print goods for that many people, but mostly it's energy. There's nothing that Earth could produce with one of these that they couldn't make far, far more efficiently without it."

"Precious historical artefacts," Ruby points out. "Instead of sending fragile things between museums in foldgates, just make a copy while sending them. Print one for every museum. Worried about them degrading over time? Print a new one from the data later. Ultimate storage."

"Well, okay, it could have that one specific niche use, but in general the energy – "

"Printing people."

"People on Earth have no problem making people as it is. But man, can you imagine the social chaos? This thing would be outlawed everywhere immediately."

"The wealthy would make copies of themselves as a way to cheat death. That'd be like a service, I bet, a special kind of life insurance. $100,000 per year and we'll keep a copy of you in reserve to reprint when you die. Come make a new copy every six months."

"People would train up one worker and make copies."

"We already do that."

"Yeah but they'd do it in a creepy corporate way, probably to prisoners or something."

"If you copied yourself and your copy killed someone, would you be liable for murder?"

"I think only the copy would, since it did it. But if you killed someone and then copied yourself, is the copy guilty?"

"It's in both of your pasts, so... yeah, I think so? It probably depends on what outcome makes the group who gets to decide the laws the most money."

If you copy yourself on Earth and then kill your copy right away, is it legally murder or suicide? Do copies have rights? I mean, everyone gets human rights, sure, but are they citizens of the country of their original?"

"Or citizens of the country they were copied in, maybe? Or are they stateless?"

"If you make copies of yourself, do they get equal share in your assets? Or does the first one out of the gate, the 'original', get everything?" I eat a forkful of rehydrated stew. "Did you come here to eat, or just to bug me?"

"Both, kind of. Bug you now, eat later. I've been looking at the water system – "

"There's no point in starting up the water system," I say wearily. It's a conversation we've had before. It's a conversation her progenitor had with my progenitor, still there in both our copied memories. "We switched over to the mechanical oxygenation systems awhile ago, yes, but it makes more sense to keep purifying our water by printing it with the foldgate. The water system is designed for thousands of people; if we're not making thousands of Kates – and we can't, we don't have the energy to print that much food – it's just not worth the work it takes to maintain."

"We could print more Kates if we weren't using the foldgate for our water, though."

"Yes, but not enough to make maintaining the water system worth it. There's been some talk about setting up a smaller water distillery, when we have time."

"Sooo," Ruby says in a kind of teasing tone that makes me immediately suspicious, "you're saying that if I'd been down there looking at the condition of the old pipes and soforth, I've been wasting my time?"

"Yes, Ruby, you've been wasting – "

"Even if I found this?" She whips a capped plastic tube out of her pocket and plonks it on the table in front of my food.

I stare, mouth open.

It's water. Gross water, obviously. Probably swimming with dangerous bacteria after sitting stagnant in a pipe for literal decades, although given that there's no animals or anything to shit in the pipe, maybe not. Whatever. That doesn't matter.

What matters is that it's green.

"It's green," I say, like there's some chance that Ruby hasn't noticed.

"Yep."

"Wh... what is it?"

She shrugs. "Haven't checked yet. Algae is the obvious possibility. But the point is – "

"That it's green."

"Yeah."

"There's photosynthetic life here."

"Yeah."

"How?!"

"I imagine it was probably contamination on the pipes when they were brought from Earth. Leave it alone long enough under the dim electric lighting on the outskirts where no one goes, and... well."

"Is it edible?"

"That's the main question, isn't it?" she grins. "I have no idea. I'm going to get some chemists to screen it for common toxins, and then I guess we'll see."

"We'll see? How? Even if they don't find anything – "

"Then unless we can positively identify exactly what it is, we can't be sure. I know. But it's a start, isn't it? I mean, even if it isn't edible, breeding it up under the lights can reduce strain on the oxygenation systems."

We look up as someone new enters the mess hall, but it's just Original Kate (well, a reprint of... it's kind of complicated), flanked by two older Kates. I don't really know her, except in the way that you could say all Kates know each other through our shared history. She was printed shortly before me and badly scarred in some kind of industrial accident shortly after, so she's generally escorted everywhere by her overprotective friends. They're hardly likely to come over and talk to us, so we go back to our conversation.

"If we can grow our own food..." I say.

"I know!"

"Even if it's not complete nutrition, even if it's just a supplemental food source – "

"I know! It's not like we're lacking the facilities to grow food in a colony designed to support thousands. Just something to grow. And now, we might have it."

"This could be fantastic news. But why are you telling me?"

"I had to tell someone."

"You're not going to tell everyone?"

"Of course not! You know these people. They're us. Can you imagine the absolutely fucking stupid things that a not insignificant proportion of Kates would do, jumping the gun on something like this?"

"Shove a bunch of raw algae into their mouths and die immediately, probably."

"Exactly. Safety tests first. Then I'll break the news, when I have all the data. You can keep a secret, right?"

"You know perfectly well that I can. After all, you can. Except for telling me, I guess."

"Well, you can do the same thing and tell me," she says magnanimously. "Now, if you'll excuse me, I need to go and find the most discreet chemist we have."

• • • •

<u>KATE-2-9-2</u>

"So, basically," Dani says, "we're fucked."

I sigh, and rub my temples. It's not like the answer was unexpected. I've been the head nuclear engineer of Kateopolis for over a decade, which isn't long enough to become actually good at maintaining a nuclear reactor with no specialists and no training and just the most dense operating manuals you've ever seen in your life, but it's long enough to get a pretty good sense of when you're fucked. I glance from Dani to the other Kate in the room, the one I don't know that well who was sent down from Logistics. She doesn't look surprised, either.

"The energy output is already twenty five per cent less than what it's meant to be," she says. "Is it going to get worse?"

"Does it even matter?" I ask. "Aren't we fucked either way?" That's twenty five per cent less food, less water, less medicine, less replacement hardware and clothes and general life necessities. I'm not in logistics and even I know that that's cutting things way too close to the bone.

"In theory, it's survivable," Logistics Kate says. "We distil our water, cut back all luxuries, drop our calorie input, and put a strict ban on printing any new Kates, and as the older ones die off we can loosen the restrictions. But it'd be miserable, and permanently limit our population size. And if the power drop gets worse, we won't have enough to support ourselves. So..."

"It's going to get worse," Dani says. "A control arm has broken and everything inside the reactor is very slightly out of alignment. It can't correct."

"Is there going to be some kind of meltdown or explosion or something?"

I shake my head. "This isn't the twentieth century. That reactor is pumping out a lot more power for a lot longer with a lot less matter, but if the reaction is interrupted, it fizzles out. It can't run away with itself. It needs perfect alignment or we get problems like this. So we have to fix it."

"Mitzy," Dani says in her 'seriously we are fucked' voice.

"Hmm?" I ask.

"Mitzy, it... it's an internal control arm."

I swear. Logistics Kate looks worried.

"You can fix it, right?"

What part of 'we're fucked' doesn't she understand? "Oh, yeah," I say. "We can fix it. It'll mean shutting the reactor down, sending someone in with a replacement, bolting it into place; a ten or fifteen minute job. We start the reactor up again and we should be at full power. We can even put our broken control arm through the foldgate to turn it into a new spare arm; we copied all of our critical replacement parts into the foldfield ages ago."

"Then what's the –?"

"The problem," I say, "is that, once again, this isn't the twentieth century. The startup process for this kind of reactor is very, very long, and we'd be on battery power the whole time."

"How long?"

"Two months."

Logistics Kate stares. "Two *months*?!"

"Yeah, it's a long and complicated process. And I'm guessing we can't keep the machines running that long on battery power."

Logistics Kate shrugs. "Most of them aren't a problem. This place was designed with the expectation of temporary problems like this, but it was also designed with the expectation of contact with Earth to resupply us in an emergency. The oxygen, lights, heating, all of those systems can run on battery power for six months, and we can rig up distilleries for our water needs. The problem is food. We could run the lights and water cycling for the farms on battery power, but it's not nearly enough for the foldgate, not in the rigged-up, off-spec way that we use it. For this many Kates, we have 2 weeks' worth of food stored, perhaps. If we had more time, some warning, while we were at full power, then we could print more reserves, but at three quarter power we simply don't have that kind of leeway. We have two weeks and then we start starving."

"What kind of civilisation can only feed its populous for *two weeks* in an emergency?!" Dani asks.

"Believe me, I've said the same thing many times. But the higher-ups insist on shaving things close to the bone. The more Kates, the less work anyone has to do, and we've been taking too many risks with our population. And now we have to pay for it."

"So we sacrifice some Kates now or we all starve later? Is that what you're going to propose to them?"

"If you have a third option, I'd love to hear it."

"I have a third option," I break in. I definitely don't like the third option, but I have it. I take a deep breath and force myself to speak. "It'll only take two months to power it up if we power it down. In theory, if someone knew what they were doing..." I swallow. "I could get in there and change the arm while it was active. It would take two minutes."

"Mitzy, no," Dani says.

"It's got to be done, and it's my responsibility." The steel in my voice surprises me. I'm not the self-sacrificial type, on the whole. But then, this is really sacrificing one of me to save hundreds of me, right? It's actually very selfish. Mathematically.

"Would you survive?" Logistics Kate asks.

"Long enough to do the job? Yes."

"Long enough to get out?"

"... There's a possibility, yes."

"Yeah, but you wouldn't be okay," Dani says. "You could wear all the radiation protection we have and you're still going to be cooked alive in there. If you do get out, you'll just die over several hours instead of a few minutes."

"It has to be done, Dani."

Logistics Kate shakes her head. "That's not acceptable. Your expertise about the reactor is far too important; you know more than anyone else. Send one of your lackeys."

"No," Dani and I say together.

"There's the obvious solution," Dani says. "She could just –
"

"No," Logistics Kate says.

"It'd be simple! She goes and makes a copy of herself now and sends the copy. It'd cost us nothing but a single copy run!"

"It would cost us a new Kate."

"Oh, so you're happy for one of us lackey techs to go, but not a copy of Mitzy? Then I'll copy myself and send her – "

"No!"

"What's the difference? Other than by not copying ourselves, we lose someone permanently?"

"The difference is precedent," Logistics Kate snaps. "If we do this, make a sacrificial Kate to deal with this issue, where does it stop? We both know – we all know – where that slippery slope leads."

"How many reactor issues with no backup food stores do you expect to encounter? As soon as we've solve this, people will begin preparing – "

"The reactor isn't the only piece of critical hardware in this colony. What happens when one of the domes is badly damaged, and needs risky outside repairs? When buildings collapse? When we encounter something that might be poisonous and we want to test it? You know perfectly well that if we begin on this path, making copies of ourselves designed to die, there's no telling where it ends."

"So you'd rather kill someone without a recent copy? That's worse than – !"

"It's not necessary," I cut in. "You're both missing the obvious solution here." I swallow again, and force myself to continue. "I'll copy myself, and then I'll go and do the repair. The copy will take my place as head nuclear tech."

"How is that any different?" Dani asks. "The order we come out of the foldgate doesn't actually make us more or less original than – "

"It's different," Logistics Kate said quietly, "for the same reason you protested her sacrificing herself but were happy to send her clone. We can talk about the physics of it all you want, but the way we feel walking into the gate, the way we treat each other, is that the one who walks out is the original, yes? I think this will work. I think we can get it done, have a head tech, and avoid setting a bad precedent."

"We need to gather the Kates in charge and pass this as a law," I say, trying not to sound how I feel, like I've just jumped off a cliff. I'm going to die. I'm actually going to die. "Make this the new rule. We don't make copies to sacrifice – if sacrifices have to be made and we copy ourselves, the original makes the sacrifice."

"They won't agree to that," Dani snaps.

"Yes, they will," Logistics Kate says, "because the alternative is mass starvation."

"There has to be another way. I still think this sets the bad precedent; we – "

"No, it doesn't," Logistics Kate says, "because no matter what the physics says, you believe the original is the original. It's obvious from how willing you were to send a copy, but you're fighting tooth and nail to stop your boss from going and leaving a copy in her place."

I don't hear the rest of their argument; I'm already heading to the town centre. Heading out to propose the law. And have it agreed to. And copy myself.

And die a painful death to save hundreds of myself. Like the selfish bitch I'm trying desperately to tell myself I am.

• • • •

KATE-2-9-2-1

There's dirt in the box.

There's dirt in the box, and I have never been so happy to feel it there. Because that means that I'm not Mitzy. I'm her copy, the new fuel tech printed after she fixed the reactor. I'm alive! I get to live! I'm already sobbing before I realise how weak and stupid that's going to make me look to the other Kates, but right now, I don't care, because there's dirt in the box. I'm not the original.

I push the box open, but Kate-4 isn't waiting for me. Dani is. And she looks grim.

"Hey, Mitzy," she says.

"Hi," I say. "But I do need to pick a new name." I indicate the box. "Tradition, and all that. Not being the original."

"Yeah, about that. Uh. We have a problem."

"A... problem?"

"Mitzy... didn't manage to complete the repair. The bolts were stuck, it took longer than expected. She was... she..." Dani swallows. "It's mostly done now, but if it's not completed within the next few hours, we have to shut the reactor down. So... we need you to try again."

"I... I don't... the whole point was not to send copies..."

"And that sounded like a great idea at the time, but we're on a very limited timeframe and you are the one with the skill to best pull off this job." She tries a smile. It's not very reassuring. "You volunteered once. We need you to volunteer again."

• • • •

KATE-2-9-2-2

There's dirt in the box.

There's dirt in the box, and I have never been so happy to feel it there. Because that means that I'm not Mitzy. I'm her copy, the new fuel tech printed after she fixed the reactor. I'm alive! I get to live! I'm already sobbing before I realise how weak and stupid that's going to make me look to the other Kates, but right now, I don't care, because there's dirt in the box. I'm not the original.

I push the box open, but Kate-4 isn't waiting for me. Dani is. And she looks grim.

• • • •

KATE-2-9-2-3

There's dirt in the box.

There's dirt in the box, and I have never been so happy to feel it there. Because that means that I'm not Mitzy. I'm her copy, the new fuel tech printed after she fixed the reactor. I'm alive! I get to live! I'm already sobbing before I realise how weak and stupid that's going to make me look to the other Kates, but right now, I don't care, because there's dirt in the box. I'm not the original.

I push the box open, but Kate-4 isn't waiting for me. Dani is. And she looks grim.

• • • •

KATE-2-9-2-4

There's dirt in the box.

There's dirt in the box, and I have never been so happy to feel it there. Because that means that I'm not Mitzy. I'm her copy, the new fuel tech printed after she fixed the reactor. I'm alive! I get to live! I'm already sobbing before I realise how weak and stupid that's going to make me look to the other Kates, but right now, I don't care, because there's dirt in the box. I'm not the original.

I push the box open, and Kate-4 is waiting for me. "Welcome to Kateopolis, population: Kate," she says. And I laugh. In the moment, it's the funniest like I've ever heard in my life.

I hope my original didn't suffer too badly repairing the reactor. I feel kind of bad about my relief at not being her. But it is what it is, and I'm not going to die.

Whistling, I stroll out of the building and get to work.

• • • •

KATE-3-5-2-1

"Now, there's an idea," Ruby says, pointing with her fork across the mess hall at the head reactor tech who'd just walked in. "Die saving Kateopolis. Get treated like a hero forever. Nice gig."

"She still has her actual gig, with the reactor," I point out. We've been doing this for nearly ten years now, and she's as random as ever. "And anyway, you'd have to die if you did that. Let your copy reap all the benefits."

"You know that it's the same – "

"Yeah, yeah, I know." I poke at my food. Ruby, I notice, isn't poking at hers.

"Not hungry?" I ask.

"Not really."

"You weren't hungry yesterday, either."

She shrugs. "Yeah, I'm sure it'll pass."

"The lack of appetite? We love eating! You might be sick."

"I'm sure I'm fine. I just." She goes to get up, then sits back down again heavily, putting her head in her hands.

"Doctor! Now!"

• • • •

<u>KATE-3-4-4-2</u>

I look down at our oncologist and purse my lips. She's unconscious now, but our interview was enlightening. The blood tests were even more enlightening.

"Is she going to be alright?" one of the Kates in the room asks. Her friend, the one who'd brought her in. An engineer, I think, and she looks barely ten years old. (Ten years older than we were when we got stranded here, I mean.) The other Kate in the room, the head of logistics, is much older, and the worry in her eyes has nothing to do with the Kate on the bed and everything to do with the fact that she's our oncologist.

"No," I say, not bothering to sugar-coat the truth. "No, she's not. Her liver's completely shot. I give her three months, tops."

"When was her last copy made?" Logistics Kate asks.

"Six months ago."

"Right, so can print – "

"It's not that simple," I cut in. "Sure, you can print as many new oncologists as you need with her skills from six months ago, but they're only going to live about nine months. Maybe a bit longer with a controlled diet, but." I shrug. "We don't really have the food source variety or purity to closely control a diet here."

"The damage was done longer than six months ago?" Logistics Kate asks.

I nod. "She says that quite some time ago, she found algae growing in the old water pipes and proposed having it tested as a possible food source. After the various poison tests came back inconclusive and trials on Kate volunteers were denied, she apparently began secretly testing it on herself."

"What?" Friend Kate gasps. "That was ages ago! That was way back just after I was copied!"

"How long ago was that?" I ask.

"I don't know, about ten years?"

"If she proposed a test and it was denied," Logistics Kate says, "I can look the exact date up in the records. Is it important?"

"The exact date? Not particularly. But I'd estimate that this damage became irreversible around six months into her experiment. So if you want an oncologist that's not on a very limited clock of her own, you need to go back at least that far."

"She knew so much less, then. We have Kates that need her *now*."

I shrug. "I don't know what to tell you. Most of her is fine, but her liver's shot. If you want someone with a working liver, you've got to go back to before it was shot. I'm surprised she survived this long with so few symptoms, actually."

"Hmm." Logistics Kate rubs her chin thoughtfully. "We could print a recent copy and an early copy, have the recent copy bridge the knowledge gap while she trains the early copy as quickly as possible..."

"What are you talking about?" Friend Kate snaps. "You're going to let her die, and print a copy of her destined to die in six months? The whole reason we have an oncologist is to deal with our old-age predisposition to cancer and extend the lives of our oldest Kates; how does printing Kates specifically to die young help?"

"Because one oncologist Kate can extend the lives of many other Kates," Logistics Kate says. "If you have a better idea, I would love to hear it."

Friend Kate looks to me. "You're a doctor. Can't you do... dialysis and stuff? To keep her alive?"

"We don't have a dialysis machine lying around. Most of the colony's medical facilities weren't transported here before the foldgate collapsed. I'm sure the engineers can use their ingenuity and the foldgate to invent one, if given time, but before she dies? No."

"Well we have to do someth – "

"Do we have the tools for surgery?" Logistics Kate cuts in.

"Um. Yes," I say. "We've done some dental work and remove tonsils and stuff. The sterile, disposable tools are all copied into the foldfield. But you're not suggesting surgery in this case, are you?"

"I am. We have a perfectly good oncologist here who needs a new liver. There are two ways past this – either we lose nearly ten years' worth of expertise that our other Kates need now, or we fix this one's liver, copy her data, and scrap all the liver-damaged copy data. Then we can print from this healthy, experienced oncologist as much as we need, as planned."

"I'm not a surgeon! None of us are surgeons!"

"You said you'd removed tonsils, right?"

"That's not comparable on any level to a liver transplant!"

"But she'll die anyway if you don't do it, right?" Friend Kate cut in. "And so will any other oncologists that get printed with enough knowledge to be useful. So what have we got to lose by trying?"

"True," I concede, "except for the obvious point, which is that as much as we joke about this being a post-scarcity society, we don't have a bunch of healthy livers sitting around for transplant."

"We have two hundred and nineteen healthy livers sitting around for transplant," Logistics Kate says.

I stare at her. Then I look down at my patient.

""We'll need a volunteer," Friend Kate says. There's a little tremble in her voice, and I don't know her at all, but I know myself well enough to read what she's thinking. She's wondering whether she's going to have to volunteer herself. "We find someone who'll do it, then copy them so we can print a replacement, then we – "

"Um," I say. "Actually. None of us are likely to have great livers at this point. I mean, nobody seems to have any major problems, except this one, but our diets and the impurities native to our air cycling system take their toll. Our best option would be to find someone who's spent as little time in Kateopolis as possible."

"A really early, fresh print," Logistics Kate translates.

"Yes."

She narrows her eyes. "We have a law about this. Kates who are sacrificed choose it themselves. We don't make disposable copies. The precedent would – "

"Look," I say. "Do you want a healthy oncologist or not? And honestly, I think it's much crueller to make someone choose to die, to have them know they're about to die, than the alternative. I'm just the doctor, and this is my medical advice.

You want me to try my hand at replacing a fucking organ? I can't guarantee success, but bring me the organ and I'll try. You want the best chance of success? The best chance is with a young liver. What you do with this information is up to you."

. . . .

<u>KATE-8</u>

Waking up inside a cramped, dark metal box is somehow even more disconcerting the second time.

There are extenuating circumstances, I suppose. My five companions are long dead, meaning there's no particular rush to get up before properly reflecting on my situation, and the fact that I made this journey through a collapsed foldgate isn't helping.

Also, there's a bunch of dirt in the box with me that wasn't here when I went in. I'm not sure what that means but it's probably really bad.

Fortunately, I'm a fucking genius. I mean, I'm *by definition* the best foldgate tech on the planet, so. That has to count for something. Right?

I... seem to be fine. Except the dirt. I'm not happy about the dirt. That wasn't in the box when I went in, meaning there's something wrong with the data, meaning there could be all kinds of shit inside me. I'm going to have to run as many medical tests as possible. As soon as possible.

I push the lid of the metal box up and go to climb out into the empty, desolate transport room.

It's not empty.

"Welcome to Kateopolis," the older woman standing over me says, giving me a gentle smile. "Population: Kate."

She looks like me (obviously, there's no one else here), except about fifty years old. My first thought is a somewhat delirious, 'oh, I guess it took a really long time to perfect this tech, then'. But as she helps me out of the box, I can see that this place has undergone a lot of changes; foldgate boxes are piled in neat stacks in one corner, crates of apparently random goods in another, and a big chart on the wall is covered in names of things with values and little ticks next to them.

"What's going on?" I ask.

"All in good time," the older Kate says, pressing a cup of water into my hand. "You need to get your fluids up and get some rest."

I drink it in three gulps. It tastes strange, a little tangy. There must be blood in my mouth or something. Older Kate takes a seat in an office chair that's seated behind one of several desks against one wall, and gestures to another. I sit down.

"So," she says. "Let's start by answering your questions."

I have questions. I have a lot of questions. Kateopolis has been around for a lot longer than I ever would've expected to survive out here, so far from Earth – it's a little overwhelming. But I only get through a tiny fraction of the questions I want to ask before a sudden wave of fatigue overcomes me.

"Are you alright?" Older Kate asks me, frowning. "The printing process can be pretty exhausting... come on, let's get you to bed."

. . . .

<u>KATE-3-4-4-2</u>

I look down at our oncologist and purse my lips. Then I look at the much younger Kate lying next to her, sleeping peacefully. Fuck, we were so young when we came here.

I try to remember everything I'd read, all the educational videos I'd watched, all the simulations we'd done, as I pick up my scalpel. My hand isn't shaking, so that's a start.

I'm not a fucking surgeon. But I guess I am now.

I glance at my assistant. Barely any of her is visible behind the mask and hairnet, but her steady eyes meet mine.

"We'd better get this right," she tells me. "The consequences if we don't..."

"I know," I nod. "If we don't get this right, Kateopolis will be without experienced oncologists."

My assistant shakes her head. "If we don't get this right," she tells me, "They'll print a new oncologist and a new organ donor, and make us keep trying until we do."

COPY<|>PASTE 3: Intrapersonal Conflict

KATE-4

We older Kates saw the crisis coming long before the younger ones did, I think.

Well, that's not necessarily accurate. I think everyone knew that if we managed t maintain a decent life expectancy, we were going to hit a critical point where the older Kates couldn't work and our population and resource limits would force a lot more labour on the youngsters until us older ones started dying off to make room for replacements. It's fairly obvious when you think about it, and we have a whole logistics division for thinking about this sort of thing.

But us older Kates paid more attention. To the youngsters, it was some far-off thing that would hit eventually. To us, well, whenever a joint became a little harder to bend, a limb became a little more painful to move, a sense became a little duller, we were aware of the ticking clock. And we knew that eventually, when the youngsters decided the situation was untenable, a decision would be made, and it would be our arses on the line. (We know how Kates think, see.) So by the time it was decided that something must be done about the ageing population, by the time that critical vote was held, we were prepared. We'd been prepared for years.

I think the Kate across from me – Dotty, her name is – is a little surprised at just how quickly us oldies agreed on a spokesperson to send to her. She doesn't know that I was picked for this job over a year ago. Before I had to retire from foldgate duty, I'd been the first Kate that most new Kates see, and that impression goes surprisingly far. I was probably the first Kate that Dotty ever saw, although I'm not certain – I don't remember every Kate. I'd at least have been the first Kate that a couple of her Kate ancestors had seen, so the memories are there. She watches me quite coldly from the other side of the table, nevertheless.

"So," I say. "You've decided to kill us."

Pink tints her cheeks. "That's not what's happening."

"It's mass murder and you know it."

"It's a time skip! You know how we do things. The Kate that comes out first, the one from making the copy, is the one who made the copy. If we put you through and pause – "

"Don't you go lecturing me of all people on how printing Kates works! You want to put us in that gate, let it dissolve us, and not pull us out the other side. We call that murder."

"By that logic, it's murder every time we copy someone. It won't be forever. Those of you who go in will be reprinted when there's space for – "

"That's never going to happen and you know it. You can make all the promises and draw up all the charters you want, but we both know that when there's room for more Kates, nobody's going to be printing arthritic seventy-year-olds instead of fresh young engineers. We won't be doing this."

"You don't have a choice. You were outvoted. Eighty per cent of the Kates over the age of sixty five will be preserved until our capacity allows – "

"Preserved," I spit. "At least come up with a good euphemism. Like I said, we won't be doing this."

"Like I said, you don't have a choice. It's going to happen. Don't make it more unpleasant than it needs to be."

"You know, if I was still running the foldgate – "

"But you aren't. And you won't be allowed anywhere near it, unless your name is drawn for preservation and you have to go through it. Until then, this meeting – " Dotty's cut off by a sudden piercing alarm. "What's that?!"

"Well, in my vast experience at surviving inside this colony that apparently doesn't mean anything to you people, I'd have to say that that's an airlock failure alarm. Airlock two, would be my guess."

The sound grows louder and faster.

"And that would be the airlock two failure alarm and the airlock one failure alarm ringing at the same time. Oh, and... is that airlock four? It's honestly impossible to tell with them layered over each other like this. And of course, my hearing isn't what it used to be."

"What did you do?!"

"Me? I've been sitting here talking to you. Some of the other oldies might have taken matters more directly into their own hands." I smirk. "Oh, don't look so worried – the colony isn't exposed to the outside. Those alarms just mean that one of the airlock doors has failed. Each airlock has a second door that's working fine. It wouldn't be an airlock otherwise."

Glaring at me, Dotty picks up her radio and calls security to warn them of the situation. I don't try to stop her. There'd be no point – the safety and security teams presumably know what all the alarms mean (I don't; I'm just bluffing based on my knowledge of the plan) and have already sent people to deal with the problems. It'll take them a few minutes to get to the airlocks all ready to arrest the saboteurs only to find out that it's the outer airlock doors that have been sabotaged, not the inner ones, and that the Kates responsible are all outside the protective dome of the colony in space suits, ready to blow the inner doors on command and completely untouchable without opening an inner door and contaminating the colony with the toxic atmosphere outside. Someone might suggest taking the risk anyway (better a small atmospheric contamination than the whole colony being destroyed), and at that point they'd need time to learn that the entire colony was mysteriously devoid of space suits (the couple we'd kept inside for an emergency were far too well concealed for them to find any time soon), and that all the space suit printing data had been scrubbed from the foldgate months before they'd started throwing this 'preservation' plan around and started guarding the foldgate from us old folks.

We really have been preparing for this sort of thing for quite some time.

I know how Kates think. I know they won't be ready to consider our demands until they realise that they're screwed otherwise. Making demands while they think they're safe is a waste of time, so I wait through Dotty's little talk on the radio, and I wait while she runs out of the room, and I amuse myself with a couple of rounds of solitaire using the deck I'd brought until she eventually comes back.

"Is this really what you want?" she snaps.

"I think what's more important is what you want," I reply. "Your side of the vote won. Is this really what you want? We'd love to live out our lives in a nice, non-destroyed colony, but your plan doesn't really allow for that, now, does it?" I frown at my Solitaire game. I really need the three of clubs, and I can't find it.

"You won't do it," I say. "You were one of the first Kates. You've been here since the beginning. You won't destroy everything and everyone in a stupid, petty – "

"Fight for survival?" I peek under the hidden cards until I find the three of clubs and add it to my deck. "Come on, Dotty. You know us, because we're you. So think carefully." I put my three down, and put a two and an ace on top of it to complete the set. "What would you do, in our situation?"

"What do you want?" she asks wearily.

"Apart from not dying?"

"Yes, apart from that."

"Just the ability to make sure you won't be able to kill us."

"Which entails what, exactly?"

With that pesky three dealt with, finishing the game is easy. I sweep my cards up. "Kateopolis is about to become a glorious theocracy," I grin. "The foldgate brings us life and the foldgate sustains life. All praise to the gate, a device so powerful and sacred that only the most venerated elders may tend it."

Despite the stakes of the situation, Dotty rolls her eyes at my theatrics. "You want control of the foldgate."

"Yep. The central logistics offices belong to us now. Nobody under the age of sixty five may enter, unless being escorted by one of us for copying purposes. You want stuff printed, it goes through the senior citizens. You want stuff copied, it goes through the senior citizens."

"You realise that this isn't just about new Kates. You're talking about taking full control of our food, hardware, and medicine supply lines."

"Yep!"

Dotty narrows her eyes. "The others would never go for this."

"Then I suggest that you remind the others how hard it will become to breathe once the inner airlock doors are breached… oh, and that the Kates outside have a limited air supply in their space suits. They're waiting right now, ready to repair the breached doors as soon as they receive the right code, but if they run out of time, they'll simply blow the doors." I pocket my cards and stand up. "So I'd work quickly, if I were you."

• • • •

<u>KATE-3-2-3-1</u>

I drop in to see my favourite artisan on the way to the community meeting. "Lonnie. Hi."

She doesn't look up from the glass lens she's polishing. "Your new lenses are going to be late."

"I can see that." The artisans are some of the most important Kates – they make things. If there's some piece of equipment that we need that isn't in storage and hasn't been copied into the foldgate, an artisan will craft the most perfect version they can to copy it in. Sometimes, this means carefully leaching heavy metals from the soil outside the domes. Sometimes it means mixing new flavour combinations for foods, or carefully soldering electronics. Today, for Lonnie, it means hand-grinding a specific lens of a size and magnification that we don't have in storage, so that me and the other meteorologists can look at some high-activity radioactive dust clouds and determine if they're a danger to Kateopolis. "It's no rush," I assure her. "The cloud is weeks out. What caused the delay?"

"I had to teach a group of Kates how to sew a button properly."

"Ah." That makes sense. In the year or so since the older Kates took over the foldgate, there's been a lot more DIY. In the old days, if we broke a button, we'd just print a new shirt, but people don't like using the foldgate any more. Handing the materials over and meekly explaining to an old lady what you want feels... like more of an imposition, I guess. It makes you second-guess whether it's worth their time to copy.

"I have more exciting news than some cloud, anyway," I grin. "You'll never guess what our astrophysics department discovered."

"That a meteor is going to crash here and kill us all?"

"Something much less important. But also, much less boring. We know what caused the foldgate to collapse in the first place."

That, finally, gets Lonnie to look up from the lens. "You discovered what cut us off from Earth?"

"Yep! The short answer is, solar flares."

"Electromagnetism doesn't affect foldfields, you know that. Using them in space would be impossible if it did. I know our gate is old, but this sort of thing was extensively tested long before they launched it."

"Of course it was. Electromagnetism and radiation interference and distance and relative velocity of the two gates and all that were ironed out long before we were born, but on Earth they didn't know – they had no way of knowing – that a moderate-to-severe white star solar flare, when filtered through an 0.5atm atmosphere rich in uranium and non-oxygenated iron dust, can stimulate the uranium to cause foldfield interference. And that, we think, is what happened the first time one of our semi-regular solar flares hit. The foldgate itself was in an Earth atmosphere beneath our shielded dome far enough away from the edge that we had enough of the field left to create our little loop, but the connection to Earth passes through quite a lot of the atmosphere outside our little dome."

"That's... a specific circumstance."

I shrug. "They sent a lot of foldgates to a lot of planets. Some of them were bound to fail for specific reasons that nobody thought to test. Anyway, I've got a community meeting to get to; you coming?"

"No. If they need anything weird made, they'll tell me."

"You know, if you show up to these things, you get to help decide what weird – "

"I don't care."

• • • •

KATE-7

As usual, they're a bit nervous around me at the community meeting. They always have been – they never stop seeing me as the Original Kate, after all – but it's become worse since the elder takeover of the foldgate. Technically, I'm too young to be one of the elders, by just a little bit, but they claimed me, anyway. Of course they did. They're too married to the idea that I'm somehow the oldest Kate not to. And of course, I'm the one that always gets sent as a representative to these meetings, to talk to the younger Kates. Of course.

I barely listen as the Kates go through the usual issues and cover recent problems. None of this is my problem unless they need the foldgate, and if anyone did, they'd have come to me before the meeting. The discovery of why the foldfield connecting us to Earth collapsed is interesting, but just trivia at this point – we can't re-establish the connection, so it's not like it's actionable. The Kate who brings it to our attention shares a lot of complicated math about just how far the effect of these flare-stimulated interferences can spread beyond the uranium particles and points out that it can penetrate the space suits of Kates doing outside work at the wrong time, but since foldfield interference doesn't affect human biology in any known way, this doesn't actually matter.

Finally, it's my turn to share news. I have two things to share today – one that they'll like, and one that they'll really, really hate.

I start with the good news. "The logistics team has reviewed our resource consumption, and decided there's enough room to revive three new Kates. They'll expect your decisions by the next meeting."

A flurry of discussion. I don't bother listening. It's the same every time; a talk of what industries are under- or overstaffed, the best allocation or resources and expertise... and the undercurrent that nobody actually says out loud, which is 'how old are our candidates'? Older Kates are more useful Kates, Kates with more expertise (up to a certain point; too old and they become less useful). But older Kates are also around less before they gain access to the foldgate, and have less years of useful work in them. Foldgate Kates still work normal jobs for as long as their bodies will let us, but everyone weakens eventually, and to the younger Kates, it's not just a question of 'how useful is a potential new Kate?', it's also 'will this Kate retire before I do?' There are too many old Kates now, they think, draining resources and taking up a space that could be taken up by a more useful Kate, and they're waiting for us to die off. They want a more even spread, a small old population and as big a working population as possible, so that they don't have to do as much work themselves. Printing Kates older than them is, in a selfishly practical way, counterproductive – each Kate wants to retire first, and have a strong population of able Kates in place to keep things running when they do.

So young Kates tend to be preferred these days, even though they have to be trained up again. I can already predict who they'll pick. They'll look at the tasks that most need doing, and choose the youngest Kate who has the ability to do them.

Once that conversation finishes (for the moment; the handful of Kates that actually make the decisions will discuss it casually later), I have to deliver the bad news.

"The foldfield is running out of space to store new patterns," I tell them.

There's no immediate outpouring of anger or despair. The entire room looks at me, silent. Some look worried, some thoughtful, but most vaguely bemused. It's been too many years since they were foldgate techs; they've gotten used to forgetting or ignoring the technical limitations of the device.

"That can't be right," one of them says. "When we modified that foldfield, we made sure it could store thousan – " she trails off.

I nod. The foldfield can store thousands of patterns, thousands of objects it believes to be 'in transit'. Thousands of buttons and food packets and iron gears and silicon chips and Kates. Over the decades, such things do add up.

"Many of the patterns currently stored in the field are pretty simple," I say. "The techs think we can combine some of them – rather than transporting an individual computer chip, for example, we could put together kits of a whole bunch of electronics and print a whole new kit whenever we run out of any single component. Then we can purge dozens of patterns and condense them into one. We can do this with most of our simpler specialist items, if they're small enough. Another space-saving measure that was floated is that we could store stable objects, such as metal parts, clothing and furniture, as physical objects in a warehouse and purge their patterns from the gate; then we can recopy them from the warehouse to print new ones. That idea was shot down as dangerous if something happens to the warehouse, but it's an option we have. We can also purge objects that can be simply assembled from other objects – purge all furniture, for example, and copy in wood and nails that can be used to build a wide array of furniture. However, that would involve a massive increase in physical labour to construct objects. One of the main advantages of the foldgate is how much labour it saves us. So we're not fans of that for the moment. Right now, the plan is to try the combining method, turning a lot of small simple patterns into fewer larger patterns."

"Will we need to purge anything?" a Kate asks.

"There's been some talk of purging objects that are easily constructed that we almost never need. Thus far, there's been no talk of purging any Kates. We believe that we can save enough space via the combination method that that won't be necessary for a good long time."

The room relaxes. 'A good long time' is usually taken to mean 'we don't have to worry about this, because some other fucking thing will probably kill us first'. But some other fucking thing kept not killing us first, so I make a mental note to worry about it.

Well, a mental note to expect it. I'm not worried. I don't care if we purge a bunch of Kate patterns from the foldgate. We use less than forty of them, there's no reason to hold onto the others. We could purge them all except the original, for all I care; make everyone start from scratch. Like I'd had to.

. . . .

<u>KATE-3-2-3-1</u>

The new lenses that Lonnie made for us came out top-notch. Less than a week after the town meeting, I'm tracking the approaching clouds with six new telescopes and some very fancy software that one of my techs had needed to pull up some long-buried fold tech knowledge to put together. We know exactly how dense it is, the velocity it's moving, the angle it'll hit us, and when it'll arrive. The software does the work; I almost don't need to be here at all.

There are two main reasons to track clouds like this. One: is it a danger to our dome canvas? In theory, a cloud moving with enough velocity or at the wrong angle could pose a threat to the physical integrity of Kateopolis, requiring some outlying domes to be closed off or some canvas to be reinforced until the cloud passes. We've done that before, but no dome has ever actually been breached. Which is good, because if we ever did get a hole torn in something and a bunch of highly radioactive dust thrown about to rip into everything and pile on every surface, the sheer amount of work in making that dome livable again wouldn't even bear thinking about. How would you even go about repairing, reinforcing, thoroughly cleaning and deradiating a whole fucking neighbourhood? Without extremely limited construction equipment? And while wearing space suits? If an outer dome breaches, Kateopolis will probably just write off the loss entirely.

That doesn't matter right now, because this cloud looks gentle. Very thick, but no dangerous winds. No expected problems with the dome.

The other question I need to answer is: how much fucking work will the cleanup be? Is this little annoyance going to drop a crapton of uranium and iron dust all over us that'll need to be cleaned off so that the cumulative effect of multiple clouds doesn't eventually get heavy enough to collapse the domes? And the answer to that question is, unfortunately, it's going to be a lot of work. It's a thick, slow cloud, and it's going to absolutely bury us in ferromagnetic, radioactive garbage, that a bunch of Kates (who aren't me) will have to clean off with huge brooms and shovels, in space suits. It's times like this that I'm relieved to have a cushy nerd job.

"Tansy," one of my techs calls from the door. "We've got the prediction on the next solar flare."

"That's nice," I say, not looking away from the screen. "When is it? We can use it to take some foldfield readings outside the dome and learn more about the initial collapse, if we have time."

The tech reads the date and time. I still don't look away from the screen – not because I'm not particularly interested, this time. It's because I'm also looking at the exact same date and time in my data.

"It's a really big one, this time," the tech says helpfully. "About twice the strength of normal."

I recheck my data, and realise that we're about to be under the thickest dust cloud that this planet has ever thrown at us. I stand up quickly.

"I need to run some simulations," I say, trying to keep the panic out of my voice.

• • • •

<u>KATE-4-2-2</u>

The Kate explaining the situation in our little emergency meeting is antsy, agitated, fidgeting with both hands as she paces back and forth across the room.

"We ran the simulations," she says. "Multiple times. We even ran practical experiments, using the electromagnetic emitters; they can imitate very small scale solar flares perfectly, we designed them for that to discover this phenomenon in the first place. With the thickness of the cloud and the timing of the solar flare, the foldfield disruption of the excited uranium will be far, far greater than what we normally get. I mean, I've back-calculated and found that some of the previous flares actually penetrated far deeper into Kateopolis than we expected, so – well, that doesn't matter, I guess. Important thing is, this will be the biggest foldfield disruption even we've ever seen. Much bigger than the one that collapsed our foldfield initially; that one didn't even penetrate the domes.

This one will cause disruptions for six kilometers around the cloud."

"That will penetrate every dome we have completely," one of my coworkers, Nelly, says. "Every single Kate will be within range of this interference."

"W-well, yes, but – "

"And you've said before that there weren't any known effects of this sort of disruption on Kates. Do we have new information? Are we in danger?"

"That really doesn't matter," I say. "It could give us all cancer and cook our kidneys and that wouldn't matter at this point."

Nelly frowns. "I don't understand."

"It'll reach *everything* in Kateopolis," I explain. "Every single Kate... and the foldgate." I meet the eyes of the reporting tech, and see the answer to the question I'm about to ask written there. I ask anyway. "There's no way to shield the foldgate, is there?"

She shakes her head. "We can't shield it. And the only reason we could build our little circular foldfield is that we had an untouched fragment of the original collapsed Earth field. This will obliterate that fragment. Not only will we lose the foldfield and every pattern stored inside it, but it'll also be completely impossible to rebuild it again."

Silence, for several seconds.

"What are the chances that your readings are wrong?" someone asks.

"In theory, any prediction can be wrong, but... we're more certain about this than anything we've ever reported before.

We checked many times, in as many different ways as we could."

"How long do we have?" I ask.

"Ten days, plus three to seven hours. That's as precise as the estimate can get."

"Ten days."

"Yes."

"Then let's make them count."

• • • •

KATE-9

Waking up inside a cramped, dark metal box is somehow even more disconcerting the second time.

There are extenuating circumstances, I suppose. My five companions are long dead, meaning there's no particular rush to get up before properly reflecting on my situation, and the fact that I made this journey through a collapsed foldgate isn't helping.

Also, there's a bunch of dirt in the box with me that wasn't here when I went in. I'm not sure what that means but it's probably really bad.

Fortunately, I'm a fucking genius. I mean, I'm *by definition* the best foldgate tech on the planet, so. That has to count for something. Right?

I... seem to be fine. Except the dirt. I'm not happy about the dirt. That wasn't in the box when I went in, meaning there's something wrong with the data, meaning there could be all kinds of shit inside me. I'm going to have to run as many medical tests as possible. As soon as possible.

I push the lid of the metal box up and go to climb out into the empty, desolate transport room.

It's not empty.

It's rather crowded, actually. Packed with... me. (Obviously.) Mes that look like me, and mes that don't; mes that are my age and mes that are significantly older. A Kate with a snake tattoo covering half her face and a roughly tourniqueted missing left arm offers her right hand to help me out of the box. A very old Kate in a worn and battered uniform with KATE-4, FOLDGATE MANAGER sewn on the breast gives me a smile.

"Welcome to Kateopolis," she says. "Population: Kate. For the moment."

"You're the very last one," another Kate adds. She hands me a bottle. "Have a drink."

I look around at the sea of Kates. There's a really weird vibe in the room, a sort of... expectation. Some of the Kates are wearing party hats. A lot of them are drinking. Worryingly, a not insignificant number of them are missing limbs, like the one who'd helped me up. They all look recently treated, and not particularly well – even I can see that some of them are infection risks waiting to happen. Given that I'd thought I was the original Kate up until about ten seconds ago, it's a lot to take in.

I let the feeling of *what the fuck what the fuck WHAT THE FUCK* wash over me, take a deep breath, and ask. "What the fuck?"

"We're sorry about this," another older Kate says, this one with some rather horrific facial scarring that at least looks long-healed. "It seems kind of cruel, to bring you into existence just for this, but... we kind of felt like you needed to be here. Every Kate should be here."

"It's the end of the world," says KATE-4, FOLDGATE MANAGER.

"What?" I ask. Then, to clarify, I add, "the fuck?"

"This'll be easier to show than to explain," the scarred Kate says. "How would you like a tour of Kateopolis?"

Kateopolis is beautiful, I realise as I'm lead around and shown the sights. Well, in actual fact, it's pretty ugly – many parts of it are falling to pieces, things that aren't are badly made, showing my general attitude of 'if it works I don't care what it looks like', and there's something creepy about an entire city that's full of your own face. But half an hour ago, I was eighty lightyears away from the nearest living person with no hope of ever returning to Earth, desperately refining a modified foldfield to try to make copies of myself (a terrible idea, really), wondering how long I'd even be able to keep myself alive in such a place, and now...

Banners hang between the buildings, hastily painted. HAPPY APOCALYPSE DAY, they read. Tables set up along the road display a buffet of creative treats built from deconstructing and recombining the limited array of stored foods we'd started with. Kates talk and laugh and wave and, yes, occasionally cry; many of them are already drunk and quite probably have been for days. Washing hangs on their lines, sculptures sit in their front yards. The tour takes me through laboratories and doctor's offices and warehouses and a big meeting hall. *I built this.*

Well, that's not a fair assessment. All of this was built in Kateopolis' past and in my future, in hundreds or thousands of my futures that will never happen (because I'll die pretty soon) but that already did. I'm crying a lot by the end of the tour, and only a little bit of it is because we're all about to die.

"Okay, but all of this doesn't explain one thing," I say.

"What's that?"

"Why were a bunch of Kates missing limbs and stuff?"

"Oh, that." Strangely, my guide laughs. "We ran out of calcium."

"You... what?"

"To build new Kates. We were running out of time; the foldfield could go down at any moment, and we were all very invested in having everyone be here. There wasn't time to go hauling in massive amounts of concrete or anything. So some of the Kates gave their own. Eight Kates sacrificed a limb to print you."

"Why, though? Why make me? Why bring me to life just to kill me?"

"Because you deserved to see. You deserved to be here, at the end. Every Kate does." She wipes a tear off my face with her thumb. "I was you, you know. I mean, this me, this body, was printed from the same pattern as yours. Many of these Kates are third or fourth or even fifth generation; their memories have been through the gate a few times, I'm not sure they remember the first quite so clearly."

"And you think you do?"

"No. I was printed a long, long time ago. I don't really remember what it's like to be you, either. But I remember more than they do, I think."

"Do you have a name?" I find myself asking. "I mean, I've noticed that some of these Kates have other names, so..."

She shakes her head. "They all just call me Kate. Do you want another name?"

"Uh, no. I mean, I was Kate an hour ago, and I'll be dead soon anyway, so..."

"Fair enough. Should we go and get blind fucking drunk, then?"

. . . .

KATE-3-5

I think I might be the last Kate alive.

Sandy lies with her head in my lap. With my failing strength, I run my fingers gently through her hair, but she stopped breathing several minutes ago.

When the news broke of the foldgate collapsing, we were faced with a choice. We could print as much food as possible and try to survive for as long as possible after the collapse, but nobody was interested in slowly starving to death, or in the inevitable desperate conflicts that such a famine would create first. All that pain and misery for another month or two? No thanks. Instead, we decided to go out with a bang – one last party, one night of joy, and then a peaceful, painless death. The oxygen feeds had been disconnected from the life support system sometime the day before yesterday; the carbon dioxide filters normally, but we've been breathing less and less oxygen as we use it up. Asphyxiation, as it turns out, is painless, so long as carbon dioxide doesn't build up in the body. For several hours now, Kates have been sitting down, going to sleep, and passing quietly on.

And now nobody is moving except for me.

Sandy and I were strategic about this. We're sitting on the doorstep of our old house, the one we first moved into together after falling in love. That was a few houses ago now, and a different Kate's knicknacks line the windowsills, but it has some good memories and a good vantage point for seeing the most active part of Kateopolis. I'm blinking more now, each blink is longer, and I need to decide what I want to be the last thing I ever see. Is t too cliché, to look at Sandy? Probably. But who's ever going to be able to judge me for it?

I know I'm losing it, because I see movement out of the corner of my eye. It looks like somebody in a space suit. But I must be imagining it. Nobody would be walking around in a space suit right now.

We'd all considered it, of course. At least, I'd considered it, and I assume all the other Kates had, too. In a situation like this, where everyone was asphyxiating, one could put on a space suit and simply breathe canned oxygen until all the other Kates were dead. Then one could turn the oxygen back on, and... well, with all of those dead Kates, all of that fresh meat, you could keep a very small band of you and your friends alive for a good long while, provided you could preserve it all.

I'd run the math, because it was an obvious thing to consider, but dismissed it out of hand. Eating my own corpse for several years in a big dome that was falling apart far faster than I'd be able to maintain it, with no foldgate to print new materials or resources or anything, simply didn't appeal. This way is better. Much better. Any Kate could see that.

So I must be imagining the Kate in the space suit, as I close my eyes for the last time. There's no one there. I'm the last Kate. And I am so, so tired.

We had a pretty good run, didn't we? For someone who should've died alone within weeks of the foldgate collapse. We had a really fucking good run.

Here's a fun question, Sandy. Did you believe in an afterlife? If so, do we have souls, us copies, or the copies of copies of copies? If someone travelling through a foldgate normally has a soul then someone printed in ours does; it's the same process. But we've looked through the pattern code endless times, and it's just matter, so is there one Kate soul? Are you and I going to be the same person again, Sandy, when I stop breathing? Will we still be different people, partners, or will we be one and the same again?

I can't wait to find out.

Wasting Time

When we pull into Venus port, I don't head to the hauler bar, and the rest of the crew don't ask me to. Where they turn left, I turn right, and head off among the locals. The bus I take is new; they have different restraints now. The driver, too, probably. But the route is the same as it was when I left Venus for the first time, seven years ago.

I see her before she sees me. Natalie is almost thirteen now, and oh wow, she's getting tall. She leans on the school fence, talking to a friend; both girls wear their school uniform belts at an odd angle, but it's the same off angle, so it must be the latest teen fashion or something. There is laughter in her eyes and the ugliest paint I've ever seen on her nails and crystals threaded in her hair and I'm almost surprised that I can even recognise her on sight. It has, after all, been a full year since I've seen her.

Then she catches sight of me, and her eyes light up with joy, and without even pausing to say goodbye to her friend she runs over and throws her arms around my neck (not a strain at all, she's getting so tall). "Mum!" she shrieks in delight, and pulls back a bit, smiling. "You look the same."

I nod. It's not surprising. It has, after all, only been a month since she's seen me.

"Let's get to the restaurant. We'll meet your dad there."

"Are you going to stay for my birthday?"

She always asks, and the answer is always the same. "Of course I'll be here for your birthday."

The restaurant is the same one that we always go to – my favourite, mostly because it never seems to update the décor

– and unlike Natalie, I almost don't recognise Samuel. There's new lines in his face, new grey in his hair, and he's stopped bothering to wear clothes I'd remember; only his position at our usual table, and the way Natalie rushes right over to him, tips me off that this man is my husband. I sit down, and I smile at him, and he smiles back and there's so much love there, but also tiredness. So much tiredness.

"The usual?" he asks.

"You know what I like."

We order, and Natalie orders something with Neptunian prunes in it. I frown. "You hate Neptunian prunes."

She rolls her eyes. "I love them, Mum."

"I could have sworn..."

"I think what your mother means," Samuel cut in, "is that you used to hate them when you were younger."

"Well, yeah; when I was a kid," Natalie says, and pops a prune into her mouth.

Throughout dinner, Natalie tells me about the latest fashions and the latest music and the latest drama with her friends, and I drink it all in as best I can. I'm in port for a week, and then I'm off, and by the time I get back next month this will all be a year out of date, but I try to keep up. It's all I'll have. Hair diamonds are in but hair rubies are out, if all you've got is rubies then you're best to go 'barehead' without any jewels, and Venus Fog is the latest upcoming band and Natalie thinks she'll get into acting and also I should tell dad how great it would be to get pet rats. Eventually she excuses herself to go to the bathroom, leaving Samuel and I over the scraps of our meals. I push some vegetables around my plate, not meeting his eyes, while he watches me.

"You look the same," he says.

"You always say that."

"It's always true."

"Next time I'll get a tattoo or something."

He tenses up at the phrase 'next time'. I fall silent again.

After several long, awkward seconds, I ask, "How's Valerie?"

"Fine," he says. "Valerie's doing fine."

I bite my lip, not caring if I look jealous. I'm not; really, I'm not. It would be ridiculous for me to expect Sam to wait an entire year to see me, over and over, and not have someone else. He would never have even pursued Valerie if I hadn't suggested it. It was a necessity of the situation.

And honestly, it's not even just the long waits. Sam and I had been school sweethearts and gotten married when we were both nineteen. Now I'm twenty seven, and he's... thirty five, I think? No amount of love in the world will change the fact that I am simply getting too young for him. And that's the real problem with Valerie, I guess. She's always been younger than him – two years younger. And me? Well.

"You're staying for Natalie's birthday, right?" he asks.

"Of course I'm here for Natalie's birthday. I'm always here for Natalie's birthday."

"And not much else," he mumbles under his breath, and I drop my fork and glare at him.

"What would you have me do, Sam? We have bills!"

"Everyone has bills. Everyone manages."

"If we want to get Natalie into a tier one quarternary school – "

"We both managed fine in a normal quarternary school."

" – then we need an income; a good income. Being an interstellar hauler makes me ten times the money I could make anywhere on Venus and you know it."

"Ten times the money, for twelve times the time. You realise that, right? It comes out less on our end."

"Do you need more? I can borrow from – "

"No! This isn't about needing more money; I work, Valerie works, it's fine. It's about your excuse for this job being oxshit! On our timeframe, you pull in less money this way, and you know it. You're out there on the edge of lightspeed, for a year at a time, letting it do this to you, for – "

"Do what to me? It isn't doing anything to me; I'm fine. Just because I'm living slower than you doesn't mean – "

"It's stealing time from you; time with your family! Do you see yourself? Hear yourself? To you, it's a month-on, week-off job, but every time you go out to haul near lightspeed, it's a year before we see you again."

"I understand that. I – "

"I don't think you do! I don't understand how you can – your daughter is turning thirteen! Half a year ago, she was six to you, right? In half a year for you, I raised a child into a budding teen. Six months more of this, and your daughter will be an adult. You realise that, right? In less than a year and a half, your time, *your daughter will be older than you*. And she'll barely know you! She barely knows you now! This isn't time you'll get back, you know. Once it's gone, it's gone."

"I know," I say. "I know, I just... one more haul, maybe two. Then we'll have enough for Natalie's education, and I can come back and with that nest egg I'll have time to actually spend with her, and so will you, since neither of us will have to work long hours any more. Just a couple more months, and we can – ”

Samuel reaches out and wraps his large, soft, gentle hands around mine. "Love. If you get back on that hauler ship, then when you get back, there will be divorce papers waiting for you."

Natalie comes back then, so I'm forced to bite back my reply, and I think I manage to hide my rage through dinner. Afterwards, I decide to walk back to my dorms in port rather than take the bus; maybe I can walk off some of the anger.

He doesn't understand, he really doesn't understand, how good the money is for so little time. He'd really rather I stay on Venus and work for over a decade to make what I could in a single year on the ship. And he's right, to an extent, about missing time with Natalie, but wouldn't I me missing almost as much time working long hours here? This way, I have a full week off to see her every month. And once I've made enough, I'll have as much time as I want with her.

Divorce. Ha. I should've known he'd fall more in love with Valerie in my absence. This is just an excuse.

I get to the dorms, and keep walking. Walk all the way to the hauler bar. It's full of lightspeed haulers and basically no one else but waitstaff; we haulers tend to keep to our own kind, on the whole. My crew are there, of course, as are a few other crews, all mixed up and chatting with each other, because when you've spent a month cooped up with the same people you don't want to hang out with just them on your downtime, too. We all share friendly, familiar nods and looks, friends and strangers alike. Lightspeed haulers intrinsically understand each other. There are experiences we all share that people like Samuel just don't get.

My captain presses a drink into my hands. "So your little girl's party is in three days, and then you're free, right?" he asks without preamble.

"Not so little any more. But yeah."

"You don't mind if we head out a day early, then?"

I look out the window, up through the environmental dome and toward the stars that are completely hidden by Venus' thick atmosphere. Already, I can feel the thrum of the ship's engines in my bones.

"I can be ready a day early," I say. "I don't mind at all."

Original Sin

I already know what my sentence will be, long before the judge begins to speak. In my unconquerable, relentless optimism, I imagine that there will be a miracle, that It will instead call for an immediate execution.

I'm wrong, of course. There can only be one sentence for the slaughter of a god.

"The transgressor shall be Voidcast," the judge intones, as I knew It would. "May your soul burn alone in the darkness for ten billion years where no innocent soul can witness your agony, until the merciful hand of nonexistence finally claims you."

I can't fully keep the horror from my expression. Even knowing what the sentence would be, I'd been hoping for a shorter life – a billion, maybe even just millions of years. Ten billion... but I don't fight as the guards drag me to the Circle. There's no point, and I don't want to waste my last few precious moments in the real world being in any more pain than I have to. Pain is something I will have aplenty, soon enough.

They throw me down onto the sacrificial slab, careless of how the rough rock scrapes at me. The highmage lights the flame, expression dispassionate; It has done this millions of times before, and what is one more endless torture? I go to scream the most vile string of curses I can think of, but before I can say a word, Everything is gone.

Everything

Is

Gone.

Well. Not everything. There is the all-consuming fire, eating away at all that is left of me, as it will continue to do for as long as there is anything to eat. There is my own endless screaming across the entire electromagnetic spectrum, broadcasting my agonies in ways that I am too overwhelmed to even try to control. And there are others; bright spots in the void, their own screaming visible an almost incomprehensible distance away.

We can't communicate. The distance is too great, the pain too overwhelming, and even if we could, what would there be to say? What could we tell each other that we weren't telling each other already? There is long, laborious, unrelenting pain and then there is the mercy of nonexistence. We all know this. There is nothing else.

Sometimes, one of my fellow sinners vanishes, and I am distracted for a moment by a furious envy, a rage that It has been granted the escape of an end while I still suffer. Sometimes, a new light appears in the void, and I am distracted a moment by a strange joy that another who would otherwise have lived a blissfully ignorant life will instead truly understand my pain.

I would worry that this experience was making me a worse person, except that it is already reserved for the worst of the worst.

This is how it goes, and this is how I know it will go, unchanging, until the end.

Except

Something changes.

Amidst the screams of my fellow prisoners and the debris left of long-dead former inmates, I see/hear something new.

Faint, oh so faint; I wouldn't have noticed it at all, if it weren't for the novelty.

A song.

It is nothing from any culture I recognise, but there is a rhythm to it, a declaration. Something singing that it is here and alive. Can the others hear it? I have no way to ask. To do that I would have to stop screaming, and even after billions of years, the pain is too great for that. I think it's too close, anyway; close and quiet. Somebody humming nearby. Somebody alive and not screaming. Somebody in the void who was not Voidcast.

An innocent, bearing witness? Dare I even hope?

It is hard to see anything within a limitless nothing drowned in the clamour of burning sinners, but I listen as quietly as I can. There's little else to do with my time.

The innocent is moving. Wherever It is, It's going in circles, around my general area. It takes approximately one year (the span of time that I am used to viewing as a year) to lap me once.

The innocent moves steadily. Judging by the direction from which the signal comes, It is moving in an elliptical orbit. It must be moving very, very fast, unless It is extremely close.

The innocent speaks more and more over time. A whisper becomes a murmur becomes speech, in waves of coherent light cast into the void. I do the math, I watch the direction, I notice that It is not slowed or waylaid by any other prisoner that may be in Its path. I see that It is very

very

close.

I look close, and then I see It.

It's almost on top of me! A tiny, fragile thing, clinging to a piece of debris left by – I think – my own arrival, a cast-off limb that never cast off far enough away to be gone. I cannot even see the innocent, merely hear It dwelling on the debris, and It is not shy about making its presence known. Is It trying to communicate? We have no shared language in this place, so far from reality.

I can't respond, anyway, no matter how much I try.

I watch, and I learn, and in my limitless free time with nothing else to do but burn, I learn a lot. The innocent is... strange. It is like unlike anybody I know; unlike anybody in reality, unlike the other sinners, unlike me. It is many things and one thing and It speaks in one voice of many fragmented pieces on many spectra. I do not know how It got here, I do not know where It came from

Unless

I think it came from here.

I know! Ridiculous! The void is nothing; that is its purpose! It is an unreality reserved for those who deserve far worse than a quick death, where their sins and punishments cannot impose upon the real world. Nothing can be 'from' the void! It makes no sense!

And yet, here It is. Something not Voidcast, in the void.

It feeds on me, on the fragment of offcast corpse upon which It clings. I do not resent It this; I wasn't using it, so somebody might as well. Besides, to somebody in my position, the ability to give something to anybody to benefit them in any small way is an incomparable joy. The innocent can take all of me, if that will help.

And, as I learn slowly, It is doing exactly that. It sounds impossible, but this strange being feeds on my agony.

As I scream my torment across the electromagnetic spectrum, the singer upon the debris collects it, traps it, uses it to live and to grow. Its singing strengthens, fed by my screams. My pain and my body, together, nurture this life that slowly consumes me piece by piece.

I have never been so proud in my life.

I had known since the moment that I slaughtered the god Eden that the void would be my fate. Since then, my unshaking optimism had been burned out out of me over the course of billions of years, failing me just before a miracle. I had never expected to nurture another, to be useful to anyone, ever again. But here we are.

Do the other sinners have this? Are there little singers like this elsewhere, too far away for me to hear their faint song? I have no way of asking, and the other sinners have no way of responding.

I don't know whether they have such blessings. But I know that I do.

I scream loudly and resolute, I burn as brightly as I can. I revel in my pain, knowing that every ounce of it strengthens the song of my strange voidborn child.

And for the first time ever, ten billion years doesn't seem like nearly enough time.

Isolation Hysteria

"It's called isolation hysteria," she said, placing the cup of tea in front of me, "or space madness, by people who don't like the word 'hysteria.'" She perched on the edge of the small table, leaving the chair for me. Melded with the floor as it was, the table didn't shake.

I nodded. We'd had this conversation before. "After a few months of no contact with any living thing, you'd be mad not to go mad. Hallucinate an old friend or whatever."

"What's interesting, though, is how many people don't hallucinate friends and family. Most just make someone up. Their childhood imaginary friend. The pet they always wanted. Their ideal lover." She gazed out the window at the same tiny points of light we'd been looking at for the past six months. I followed suit. No planets were close enough to see without a telescope. It was just us and the stars. The view changed as the station rotated, but not enough to tell at a glance.

"With this kind of view as inspiration, you'd think more people would hallucinate something more imaginative. Aliens or something."

"I don't think anybody believes aliens are real quite as much as they believe other humans are real."

"You have to feel sorry for the delusional when they're cured. Losing a friend, someone they relied on. Just because the delusion isn't real doesn't mean it isn't real to them."

"Who says it isn't real? Verioli posited that anything that can defend and justify its own sense of self, has a sense of self."

"Surely one could, say, program a computer to convincingly claim to have a sense of self, though?"

"Not without giving it the ability to distinguish itself from the rest of the universe and understand the power of its own actions. Verioli claimed that even a language bot capable of making those distinctions for the purposes of justifying its individuality in conversation would, by definition, have a sense of self."

"One can claim a feeling without having that feeling, though."

"Well, Verioli believed that the entire human identity was one big feedback mechanism. He thought that we analysed our own thoughts and actions after we did things and built our image of ourselves based on that; like, particularly angry people only knew they were angry because they looked at their past behaviour and it seemed angry. The evidence shows that he was right at least in terms of emotions; people often guess what emotions they felt in the past based on physical cues. A lot of people will mix up excitement, fear, and lust in their memories, because the physiological effects are so similar."

"So you're saying that we have a sense of self because we act like we do?"

"Yes. Once you recognise yourself as discreet and separate from the universe as a whole – as every decision-making creature must to survive – then the sense that this must be true follows."

"So he's basically saying that nobody really has a sense of self."

"Or that we misidentify what a 'sense of self' is." Her gaze hadn't left the window. The view hadn't changed. She seemed to have stopped blinking, but even as the thought crossed my mind, her eyes twitched closed for a moment.

I was really going to miss her.

"Maybe people should interview their delusions. See if they *can* justify their own existence."

"Wouldn't work. The delusions would give answers from the interviewer's own head."

"So if the interviewer believed the delusion had a sense of self, it'd pass."

"Waste of time, really."

"I had this one friend," I said, "who thought the self was basically an illusion, but that we should drop it to achieve enlightenment. He said that we needed to let go of our needs and desires because they anchored our thinking as individuals, and that true happiness could only be found when we let go of our narrow perspective of the self to be a proper part of the universe."

"Makes you wonder. Isn't the death of one's sense of self basically... death?"

"Would that make being cured of a delusion akin to murder?" I asked.

"I don't think so. All the components of the delusion are still in the dreamer's mind."

"But not functional. Not operating with a sense of self. If you put all of a person's thoughts into a computer that didn't operate like a human, the original person isn't there, are they?"

"Or maybe they're just changed," she countered. "Who we are changes with every thought. We don't call that 'death.'"

She suddenly leaned forward, eyes fixed on a point in space. I'd seen it, too. It's hard to miss much when all you're looking at is a vacuum with multiple light sources. The small shuttle that had just come into view was still... several minutes away? It was hard to tell the distance.

Long enough for goodbyes, before our replacement arrived to take his shift.

She finally looked away from the window, training those beautiful eyes on me. They were filled with tears. No fear, just sadness. She swallowed.

"I love you," I said gently.

"I love you, too."

"It's been great, huh? The laughter. The debates."

"No regrets, right?"

"Not until right now." I felt tears sting my own eyes. Why did this have to be so hard? It'd only been six months. Six perfect months with nobody else to talk to. The station communicator beeped. The shuttle's hailing message.

"I'm so sorry," I whispered. "More than anything, I wish you could be real."

The tears finally began to slide down her cheeks as her perfect lips twisted into a regretful smile. "I am real."

She answered the communicator, and I felt my mind begin to slide apart.

Angel

I was twenty three when the angel bit me. Stupid, really; I should have seen the danger. A figure hunched in an alley, wearing a coat too large and a scarf too fluffy for the weather, eyes constantly tracking upward to the sky. But I just thought it was some poor homeless person who might need help.

I don't even know what message the angel was carrying. It never passed it to me. I went over, calling out, and it just sat there, shivering in the alley. I'm not stupid; I stopped at the mouth of the alley, well out of reach. Or so I thought. I certainly hadn't expected the figure to launch to their feet, push themselves forward with two powerful wingbeats, and sink their teeth directly into my arm.

I know, I know; stupid. But I'd never seen an angel before! Who has, these days? I did the only sensible thing, kicking the beast off me and running home to disinfect the wound. I told myself that the transmission rate was very low. It was almost certainly fine. Almost certainly.

I didn't go to hospital. What could they have done for me, other than shut me in a small room and look on with nervous pity? No. It was probably fine. Even when the messages started singing in my mind.

It wasn't until a whole month later, when I had my parents around for dinner, that I was forced to confront the reality of my situation. My mother heard me humming the song as I cut potatoes and asked what it was. I told her it was nothing, just something I'd heard on a passing radio that was stuck in my head. Oh, what was it about? I didn't know; it was in some foreign language, wasn't sure what one.

Thinking back, I'm not sure if I genuinely believed my own explanation. But what I couldn't deny were the feathers.

They were too small for my mother to see them. I wouldn't have even noticed, if I hadn't been staring at my own knuckles, concentrating on avoiding them with the knife, but the hairs on my fingers were unusually thick and pale, a soft white down covering the flesh. I grabbed a magnifying glass and fled to the bathroom.

Yes. Feathers. Not the full, stiff bird feathers you're thinking of; these were thick hairs that split into thinner ones, fanning out into tiny, soft flat almond shapes of down. I pulled every one of them out with tweezers before returning to lunch, explaining the redness away as the effect of a new dish soap.

They were back in the morning, of course.

The growth was halfway up my hands by the time I woke up and plucked them; on the third day, it reached my wrists. By the end of the week there were fully formed feathers growing, leaving little holes in my skin where I pulled them out. I kept plucking, and took to wearing gloves.

The plucking helped. If I let the feathers be, the messages sang louder in my head, and I could feel my bones start to reshape by the time the feathers hit my elbows. Keeping the feathers back slowed the growth. Slowed, but didn't stop. By the end of the month, my gums were tender and swollen behind my teeth and the messages were singing so loudly in my head that I covered up and headed to the loudest club I could find o drown out the song. I met a nice man, Daniel, who spoke slowly and clearly when it was clear I was having trouble understanding him even in the quieter parts of the club, and I deliberately drank myself into a state where going back to his place would seem like a good idea.

With the alcohol dulling my anxiety, the song was glorious. It rolled over me in waves as I rested my head on Daniel's shoulder in the taxi home, it swelled and subdued with our movements as we discovered each other in his bed. As he lay there, restful and content, and the messages still thrummed through my skull, electrifying every nerve within me, I mused on what a pity it was that we hadn't truly shared the experience. I longed, more than anything, to share the song with him.

And I could feel the needle-like teeth pushing their way through my gums, behind my normal teeth, fresh and sharp and just long enough to cut. I ran one hand down the side of his peaceful face, and knew exactly what I had to do.

I took a taxi home. I fished the pliers out of my garage, sterilised them in vodka, and ripped the new teeth out one by one, leaving a bathroom sink full of blood and white bone needles. With every extraction, the song in my head quieted a little more until it was at its normal distracting buzz. It didn't hurt as much as you'd expect; they weren't anchored in my jaw like real teeth. It was like tearing out a row of thorns; painful, but relieving in its own way. An invader in my body gone, and when the wounds healed, all would be well.

Except I already knew that they wouldn't get the chance to heal, not properly. By morning, I could feel new teeth forming, and within two weeks, they were breaking through once more. I tore them out every time. I couldn't risk succumbing to the desire to share the song.

I still couldn't understand the messages in the song. As time went on, I could sense the shape of it, but I still didn't know what the words meant. Well, not words, the... you know what I mean. Sometimes there were smaller messages, little bits I understood; things to whisper to the pizza delivery man, to send to an old high school friend on facebook, to write among other graffiti on a wall. I never saw the eventual results of these things, but passing them on calmed the itch of the song for a little while. The big one though, the base of the whole melody, was well beyond my reach.

My arms bleed all the time now. The feathers come thick and fast and the skin can't heal before I need to pluck them again. The bathroom is full of feathers and teeth; there are too many to easily dispose of without drawing notice. Maybe there's a way to burn the feathers. I'm not sure what to do about the teeth. Bury them in the garden, perhaps?

Not that I've tended the garden in some time. I rarely go outside any more; the sky is out there, and I love it too much. It's entrancing, a home I am desperate to reach. But I suppose I should give up fighting, really. It became pointless a few days ago.

Because a few days ago, when I opened the door for the pizza delivery guy, I saw where the message is coming from.

It's a point, high in the sky. Okay, yeah; that's obvious. But I know what specific point now. I looked over the man's shoulder and, in the shifting shadows of traffic headlights, I saw the base of the ruined tower that humanity built so many generations ago to try to reach us. My predecessors struck it down and scattered them, fracturing their language into hundreds to confuse any such future coordination, and there's nothing there now, of course, but I saw it. Right under the message. Right under my home. Up there, where all languages are one, I will understand the message with perfect clarity, I will sing every syllable perfectly, I will know what it is that I am declaring and who it is for. (That's the thing that really gets me about all this; I don't know who I'm carrying this message to.) And I don't need a tower to get there. I can fly.

I locked the door behind the pizza guy and moved every piece of furniture I owned against the doors and windows to trap myself inside. But I've decided it doesn't matter. I've decided to let the feathers grow.

What else am I to do? Keep fighting to keep my arms until they get infected? Try to keep out an endless song while I dream of the sky and slowly wilt in a tomb of dead feathers? Whether I let myself change or not, the song is growing stronger, and I know where it comes from now. At some point, I will try to reach it. At some point, I will convince myself that I can, climb the highest building I can find, and jump.

When that happens, would I rather all to the pavement, a victim of my own stubborn fear of change?

Or would I rather fly?

M y imagination is starting to get out of control, I think. East is worried about me. I can see it in her eyes when we take tea this morning in the courtyard. The three of us, just East, West and I, with South off on another of your walkabouts.

I think it's a new courtyard, although I've long stopped keeping track. If I ever did keep track. How long did I keep track? Infinite courtyards in infinite houses, or one courtyard in one house; or at least four, I suppose, since four border the house, but then four houses border each courtyard, so how does one factor that, numerically? It's a matter of opinion at this point, I suppose. You can pick a direction and just start walking – house, courtyard, house, courtyard, all the same. You often do, even now, and he does it occasionally, to, although he's more interested in the eternally futile and honestly quite pointless task of mapping the world. It's not mappable. It never has been. He can break pots or mark the walls to mark his progress but it won't matter, because the house and the courtyard slowly return to their natural state over time, exactly the same as the four of us do. Put a knife through my heart and it will heal. Put a stone through the window and it will heal. I've seen enough of my own works scrawled upon the walls to know that.

It's unmappable by position, too. West has tried that, enlisting the help of the rest of us; walking away and counting how many courtyards until we meet again to estimate the size of the universe. Sometimes it takes five courtyards to meet again, sometimes twenty. Once, he disappeared for six days and counted one hundred and twenty three courtyards before running into East again in the courtyard he'd left her to mark position. West's journeys are short compared to South's, who can disappear for dozens of days at a time and then return claiming you've only been travelling in one direction. I don't know if psychology plays a part, or if you simply have a poor sense of direction.

West is present for tea this morning, although I see he's been busy in the night. Of the four gates at the four edges of the courtyard each leading to a copy of the house, the four that we whimsically named after ourselves some time ago, three gates are missing their large ornate urns. All eight urns are piled in West's gate, completely blocking it, along with many more, a massive pile of at least fifty urns, several of them already broken.

"Collecting urns?" I ask him as East collects the lifewater from the fountain to heat over the sacred flame.

He grins. "He's tracking the mess."

"The mess."

"The healing. He has a theory that it creeps in, from the edges. Remember?"

"I've heard the theory."

"Right, so. What happens if he collects the urns from all the surrounding courtyards? And keeps piling them in here, over and over? The pots should regenerate out there before they're removed from in here. So if he keeps collecting, he can increase the amount of pots!"

"Why?" she asks as the water heats, transmuting it into tea. "There's already infinite pots. We have as many pots as he could ever need."

"It's the principle of the thing." He points at me. "I get it."

"I do," I agree. If West is right... if it's possible to preserve an area against healing...

We all have our little ways of dealing with the passage of time, but I think East worries about mine the most. Mine certainly looks the strangest, I agree; it takes time and effort to develop a visual code to record thoughts outside the mind, to protect them from the foibles of memory as the mind, too, heals over time, to mark them instead in the environment and then watch as the healing landscape eats them over time, replacing scratches and scrawlings with clean, perfect walls. The worlds I build in my mind to escape the inherent limitation of the real world have gotten more complex, more intricate, more divorced from reality, over time, but I have no way to impose them on a perpetually healing landscape, or a perpetually healing body, or a perpetually healing mind. But if West is right... if we could hold territory against eternity, damage the edges of a held area enough that they are being perpetually healed, that the middle can never be touched...

East hands me my little cup, and I meet her eyes, and I see in them that she's already thought further ahead than I have, seen the futility in the attempt. I could cover every surface in this courtyard and in the four adjoining houses with frantic scrawlings from my imagination, build my deluded world concept by concept, vandalise the neighbouring courtyards and houses beyond recognition and... then what? There's limited surface area. I could write until I run out, and then it would be a war of attrition, harm against healing, and one cannot win a war of attrition against eternity. I've tried before. We've all tried before. Every day I'd have to go out and break things, with neither time nor space for more invention, protecting written ideas as they grow more and more stale and I forget why I cared so much in the first place until one morning I don't do it, just one morning, and all of my hard work vanishes in the night, rendering the hundreds of days of effort completely pointless.

I take the tea. I stare at it. I consider, for a moment, not drinking it.

We've all done that before. In every courtyard, there is the fountain, and in every courtyard, there is the firepit, and every morning, we heat the lifewater over the sacred flame and transmute it into the tea that keeps us alive one more day. But we don't have to. Sometimes, somebody will decide they've had enough and refuse to drink, and simply not wake up the next morning.

This solves nothing. We simply lie inanimate in our beds, or wherever we went to sleep, until somebody decides they're bored and wants to talk to us and trickles tea between our lips, and we wake as if no time has passed at all. South does it the most often – when you're on one of your walkabouts like this, it's a toss-up as to whether you'll walk into a courtyard with somebody else again, or whether somebody will find you passed out in some house a dozen days from now – but we've all done it. A few times, we've all done it at the same time, on the logic that there will be nobody around to rouse us. This doesn't work either – we all simply awake in our beds one morning. Maybe it's the next morning, maybe it's a thousand mornings hence – we have no way of knowing.

Once, with South's permission, West took South's comatose body and dismembered it, cutting it into the smallest pieces he could and scattering them far and wide. He wanted to see if a comatose person would still heal. They do, although we're not certain what criteria the universe uses to decide which piece to re-heal into the person and which pieces to eliminate. We did learn a lot about all the different parts inside a body, though.

In any case, on this particular morning, I drink the tea. I taste the taste. I imagine, like I do most mornings, a world where there is more than one taste.

"Imagine plants on that," East says suddenly, pointing at West's pile of urns, and I look at her in surprise. It must have been at least four or five hundred mornings ago that I'd explained my idea of plants to her, and I don't think I'd done a very good job. I'd been trying to convey the idea of an opposite world, of regression as change; I'd watched my stories erased from the wall of the courtyard and imagined it not as an absence but a growth, like something new crawling over the words and destroying them. East and I have been disagreeing on this point recently ('recently' being 'as long as I can remember'. Maybe we always have. Maybe we forget old conversations, over the thousands and millions and billions of days, and tread the same paths forever in a cycle) – the idea of creation and destruction. She views my and West's vandalism as destruction, and the healing of our environment a rebuilding. I, for my part, can't view my writing as anything but creation, and its erasure as an act of destruction. I'd built the concept of plants, a living, growing thing that eats light itself, as a sort of formulation of her perspective from mine, to try to make my point.

It had failed, of course – most of the things I say are too removed from reality for the others to make any sense of. She'd forgotten the idea immediately, so far as I'd thought, and instead I'd become fascinated with it, building it into my concept of an ideal universe.

But she had remembered, apparently.

I finish my tea. I'm usually the fastest drinker. And I propose my new bit of insanity.

"If plants were real," I say, "we could drink them."

She chokes on her own tea. "What?"

"It's this idea I've been tinkering with. The whole infinite growth thing isn't really an improvement on infinite stasis. I'm playing with the idea of... dynamic equilibrium, I guess. What if the people drink the plants to live, like we drink the tea?"

"The billions of people?"

"Yeah." I grin, remembering the first time I'd proposed to the group my radical, unbelievable idea – 'what if a fifth person existed?' South had called me an idiot and refused to engage with the idea at all. East had listened, but seemed really distressed by the idea – we already knew everyone, what could a fifth person be like? Where could they come from? Had they been hiding from us for eternity in this hypothetical, or had the universe kept them away, in other houses and courtyards, and why would that change? West, meanwhile, had gotten really confused over the idea of fitting five people in the four person houses, and how the courtyards have four sides, and started designing pentagonal house-and-courtyard arrangements. But once I could get them to understand the concept of a fifth person in my imaginary world, a hundred or a thousand or a billion wasn't any harder.

"They turn the plants into tea?"

"No, they... hmm." I hadn't thought of that. I'd envisioned them drinking the plants directly, but my imaginary world had water and fire in it – they could, theoretically, put the plants in the water and heat it. Something to think about. "Sure, maybe. The point is, they consume the plants. And the other animals. And the other animals consume the plants. And the plants eat the sunlight, it all comes back to the sunlight."

"What if they run out of plants?"

"They can't. When they don't wake up, they stay down, remember? If there aren't enough plants, there are less people." This was a big part of my imaginary world – the idea that people could both come into and go out of existence. They were created, they grew and experienced and developed things, they were destroyed. I hadn't realised it when I'd come up with the idea, but this meant that their numbers could change over time, just like the plants. "They can't be infinite people or infinite plants because they don't have infinite space."

"Because they're on the ball," West says.

"Because they're on the ball." That had been based on West's theory of the universe from awhile back. He'd posited that, since walking in one direction eventually had him wind up back in the same courtyard as the rest of us, the universe must be round. This idea had quickly been disproven (or at least rendered irrelevant, it was a little hard to disprove) by the inconsistent 'size' of said ball; there was no real way to predict how many courtyards one had to walk through to return to one's starting place. But he had salved his disappointment by helping me build a model for my imaginary world on a ball, including a daylight source outside it – rather than the universe simply lightening and darkening periodically like the real one, he came up with this idea of the ball spinning in relation to a giant firepit some distance away, so it was always night somewhere and always day somewhere. I'd found it poetic.

"And what's off the ball?" comes South's voice, causing me to jump.

"You're back!" East can't be too surprised, because she has already prepared a fourth cup of tea, which she hands over.

South nods in thanks. "What's off the ball, North?"

"The sun," I say.

"And?"

I grin. I'm proud of this part. "Other suns and other balls. Infinite ones."

"Huh. So, just like the houses and courtyards, then."

"No! No, it's not like that."

"No? Infinite suns and balls is different, somehow?"

"They're too far away. The people break, remember? They don't have enough time for things to get repetitive."

"So if they found a way off their ball – "

"Why would they want to do that?"

"If they found a way off their ball, there'd just be nothing, and they'd break before finding something that could disappoint them. Great fix."

"They wouldn't want to," I insist. "There'd be too much on the ball. They'd break before they could get bored of the ball."

"Hmm. It's a good try at any rate, North." You turn and walk out of the courtyard, into one of the copies of the house.

I throw my teacup at the fountain as hard as I can, shattering it and chipping the edge of the fountain. Aside from a slight flinch at the sound, nobody reacts much to this. Why would they? There are infinite other fountains, and this one will be fine by tomorrow. The next day, perhaps, if West's urn experiment works.

"I have some work to do," I say, and fetch a piece of coal from the firepit (ignoring the way the sacred flame burns my fingers; that, too, will heal in a day or two as if it never occurred, as if I never took this coal, as if nothing that will happen today had ever happened), and I start writing. I start writing a world too varied and intricate to ever be boring, a world of billions of minds with billions of perspectives that write billions of worlds of their own, a world of billions of sights and sounds and flavours and things that stay made and things that stay broken. I write until my fingers bleed, until I run out of coals, and West brings me a broken urn full of coals from neighbouring courtyards.

"What do I think is outside of our actual ball?" he asks.

"What?"

"Think of it. The people on the ball – if they wanted to get off, what way would they have to go?" He points up.

I look up. "There's nothing up there. Just light."

"How do we know? What if there's something behind the light? What might it be?"

"Honestly? I think it'd be more houses and courtyards."

"I'm probably right. He's off to find out!"

"How?!"

"By finding stuff he can build a ladder out of!"

"A ladder to the sky? Before it all vanishes in the night?!"

But he's already leaving.

"His task is impossible!" I call after him.

"He knows that!" he calls back.

I reach into the urn and pull out a chunk of coal. I keep drawing, I keep calculating, I keep writing.

Time will eat the marks I make. And eventually, time will eat my memories of them, too. Every day in the future, this day will have existed a little bit less, until it, like the things I wrote yesterday, and the day before, and a day two thousand days ago, might as well have never happened.

But it exists today.

Dr Simmons tapped her pen against her lip, deep in thought. Dr Wu strode across the room to stand beside her and followed her gaze through the one-way mirror.

"Still haven't cracked it?"

"It's puzzling. Everything showed a perfect memory transfer, but..." Simmons fell silent and continued to contemplate the figure on the other side. A young-looking male, muscular for a doctor, strained against the restraints holding him in his chair with a blatant disregard for the drip in his arm. The microphones were off, but he was obviously screaming profanities at the mirror. It was... disconcerting to see their proper, uptight colleague in such a state.

"... but this is the first time that a clone has actually thought that they *were* the original," Wu finished. "Have you tried communicating with 3W1 again?"

"Not since I vaccinated it this morning, but there's really no point. It just keeps begging me to believe that it's Walters and swearing at me when I don't. I'm beginning to think... well, it's a bit risky, but..."

"What?"

"She wants to send me in," Dr. Walters' voice announced. The two spun around to see him standing in the doorway. "And I agree, it's a good idea. Perhaps my presence will convince 3W1 of the truth."

"You can't come in here!" Wu protested. "We have the no-contact protocols in place for a reason. If we went around working with our own clones, that have our own memories, then – "

"I'm aware of the mental health implications, Wu, but can you tell me that it's entirely healthy for you two to be dealing with that thing either? Until we get the safety clearance to try the memory transfer on clones from the public, we're going to be working with subjects wearing the faces of our colleagues. There's no way around that. Can my contact really be any worse than you two having to deal with this every day?"

The two women looked between the collected doctor in the doorway and the struggling, screaming clone in the containment chamber that shared his face.

"A single contact attempt shouldn't have any negative effects. Let me sedate him tonight."

"Well... okay," Wu said eventually.

Dr Walters waited until his colleagues had left for the night before attempting to sedate the subject. The clone had ceased struggling; it merely glared murderously when he entered.

"How are we feeling, 3W1?"

"You son of a bitch. Do you really expect to get away with this?"

"Yes, actually, I do." The doctor smirked at the subject before turning his attention to drawing a dose of sedative. "See, the wonderful thing about you is that you take such good care of your body! Not a mole or a pimple, and you have all your major organs replaced with culture tissue regularly, using the most modern, scar-free techniques... that level of vanity can get you into trouble. Any examination would show – "

"Healthy, young tissue, as expected from a clone; yes, I got it, I'm not stupid."

"Amazing you didn't figure it out *before* the memory transfer, then. You could've at least got yourself an identifying tattoo or something. Or had somebody else set the vat locks. Uploading the lock combinations into the brain of your captive? Not a smart idea."

"The others will figure it out eventually."

"No, they won't. I have all your memories, remember? I can be you as easily as you can. And there's nothing incriminating on tape; I made sure of that." He injected the sedative into the subject's IV and reached for a second needle.

"What the hell are you doing now?!"

"Oh, this?" The doctor waved the needle. "Well, it really would be best if no suspicion was thrown on me whatsoever. So 3W1's complications aren't going to be just related to the memory transfer. It's going to suffer from heart failure as well. The failure will be a mystery that can never be solved; it might set our new memory transfer technology back a few years, but that's a necessary sacrifice for security, don't you think?"

Ignoring the way his victim strained against the restraints and swore at him, the doctor injected the serum. "And now I must get home to my family. Suzie will kill me if I'm late for dinner again, you know what she's like."

It's not impossible to live in the well.

When I fell in, a naive child committing the apparently unforgivable sin of not looking where I was going, I hit cold water and was certain, dead certain, that I was going to drown. I'd been wrong, as children often are. It's an old well, the bricks cracked and fallen in in many places, and back when the water was higher it had washed away a lot of the dirt behind the bricks, creating a little hollow where it's possible to sit, or even lie down, above the surface of the water. I'd dragged myself up and shivered myself dry and, to my surprise, survived.

After that, I'd been certain that I would be rescued. But I'd been wrong about that, too. I hadn't told anyone where I was going, and the entrance to the well is overgrown and hidden; if they looked, they probably looked in the wrong places. And they would've given up by now. It's been such a long time.

It's not so bad. There's clean water down here, and the fungus and ivy that grows even this far down is edible. Sometimes something else edible falls in the well, a rare boon. So long as I'm careful to conserve my energy, I can scrape together enough to live down here – and my little hollow of dirt (I've tried making it bigger, it's impossible, there's nothing but stone behind it) isn't big enough to do more than sit or lie down anyway, so I don't have to waste energy on exercise. There's more than just the bare necessities down here, too; I also get the glorious luxury of sunlight. In the winter, I get almost thirty minutes of direct sunlight per day as the sun passes overhead, although I often have to lean into the rain to touch it. And in the summer, almost two full hours of light a day. It's beautiful. You learn to see the beauty in light on water, when you live in a well.

But the best feature of the well, easily, absolutely no contest, is the rope.

It's old and rough and about as thick as my wrist. It hangs from the distant light above, anchored somewhere outside the well, I think, and reaches almost to the water below me. I've tried to scale the bricks enough times to be absolutely certain that that rope is the only way out of the well. Sometimes I like to hold it in my hands, feel the rough bite under the slime, and dream of where it could take me, dream of hauling myself up and out into a world of endless sunlight and cooked food and warm beds and standing room and loving family. A wonderful heaven glimpsed in the fuzzy circle of light at the top of my world and the hazy memories in the back of my mind. I am so, so lucky to have this rope, the greatest treasure of my world; a way out of it.

I've never actually tried to climb the rope, of course. It's old, it's rotten, there are frayed and frail patches high above. I think there's about a fifty per cent chance it could take my weight and lift me out, and a fifty per cent chance that it would break and drop me once again into the waters below. I'm not worried about that; I fall into the water sometimes, it's no big deal. It's easy to climb back onto my ledge. I'm not scared of a drop.

I'm scared of losing the rope.

If I try to leave and the rope breaks, I'll have no way to leave. I'd be stuck in a well with no rope out. And that would be intolerable. It's not worth it. It's not worth the risk of losing the rope. It's better to just stay here than to risk losing the way out.

If I climb the rope and it breaks, I'll be trapped forever in the well. I don't think I could live with being trapped forever in a well. Better to stay here than to risk that. Better to collect my water and scrape mushrooms off the wall for dinner and run the rope through my hands very, very carefully, so as not to break it. It's fine here in the well.

It's not impossible to live in the well.